Broken Dolls

A NOVEL

Tyrolin Puxty

CURIOSITY
QUILLS PRESS

A Division of **Whampa, LLC**
P.O. Box 2160
Reston, VA 20195
Tel/Fax: 800-998-2509
http://curiosityquills.com

© 2015 **Tyrolin Puxty**
http://www.tyrolinpuxty.com

Cover by Eugene Teplitsky
http://eugeneteplitsky.deviantart.com

Stock by Larissa Kulik
http://annmei.deviantart.com

ISBN 978-1-62007-929-4 (ebook)
ISBN 978-1-62007-930-0 (paperback)
ISBN 978-1-62007-931-7 (hardcover)

TABLE OF CONTENTS

CHAPTER ONE

BROKEN DOLLS

I don't remember being human. Probably because I don't want to. The professor tells me how cumbersome the body is and how aches and pains are a way of life. He says this way, I'll never feel any pain and can dance for as long as I like, never growing old, never damaging my joints.

He calls me his little broken doll.

I rest my hands on the professor's thumb. I'm about the size of his foot, but my arms are disproportionally small. I struggle performing mounts because I can't grip my ankles, but the professor promised he'd fix it soon.

He's holding another doll in his hands, frowning as he adds intricate details to her face. He's serious most of the time, and I have to really concentrate to hear him speak.

"You're making a new friend for me?"

"I am." I'm sure he means no offense, but his tone sounds like he isn't paying any attention to our conversation.

I lift my hands from his thumb and smooth the crinkles in my tutu. I'm wearing an orange leotard today, a color I'm not fond of. I'll be stuck with this outfit for a week until the professor sews a new one for me, but I'm not too concerned. I'll have a friend to play with, so I can overlook pretty much everything else.

Her features are coming to life. She looks a lot like me. The professor has given us both large eyes – larger than our upsettingly small hands. They're sky blue, with a white sparkle in the corner. My nose isn't as petite as hers, but it doesn't bother me. We're each pretty in our own way. Her lips are pale, and she has a dimple in her right cheek. I press my fingers into my own cheeks, the plastic unyielding. I've always wanted dimples. Maybe I can ask the professor.

Her hair remains ruffled, hanging limply by her waist. It compliments her black corset, black skirt, and black boots. Wow. She sure does go for a lot of black.

"Will you paint her lips red like mine?"

"No." He dabs his paintbrush into the ink. He's enhancing her eyelashes now. "You're a ballerina. She's a goth. Your makeup will be brighter than hers."

"Oh. Of course!" I smile, but I feel stupid. I need to learn to keep quiet when he's working.

I practice my jetés. It's freeing to leap, but not all of my joints are as flexible as they could be. I have a natural point, but my hips don't allow my leg to extend as far as the humans' on TV. They squeak every time I try. Ballerinas shouldn't squeak.

The professor leans back in his chair and crosses his arms. He beams at the goth doll staring vacantly into his eyes. "There. She's done! What do you think, Ella?"

I can't stop my chest from puffing out with excitement. I suck on my lips to contain the goofy smile spreading across my face and walk towards my new friend. I stroke her hand, waiting for a response. When nothing happens, I take a step back.

The professor grins, his glasses falling to the tip of his nose. "Don't worry, my dear, I haven't activated her yet. Should I make any other changes before I do?"

I tilt my head to the side, examining my new friend. "No, I like her. She's different than me, though. Why is she broken?"

The professor scratches his pointed chin and runs a finger through her hair. "She used to harm herself…" His tone is soft, as always, but there's a hitch in his voice. He gently taps her wrist, his nostrils flaring. "I didn't paint the scars. She doesn't need a reminder."

I glance at my knees where the hinges poke through my stockings. Should I voice the question that blares in my mind? "Wh… what did you keep me from remembering?"

He tears his gaze from the goth doll and looks at me, expressionless. I struggle reading the professor. His voice is often monotone, and he has an impressive poker face. "Why would I tell you what I'm keeping from you, if I'm keeping it from you?" he smirks and cups his hands together, indicating for me to step on. I step into his hands, his flesh bouncy. He travels slowly because he knows fast motions make me queasy. He lowers me into the treasure chest, beautifully decorated to look like my old bedroom, apparently. He leans in and gives me a kiss on the head, avoiding my carefully pinned bun. "So long as you can dance, Ella, you needn't worry about the past."

I pace in the chest. It's fairly big – probably a few human feet wide and long, but I can't be sure. Its exterior looks decrepit and rotting, but the inside is lined with plush carpet and pink wallpaper. The professor placed a mirror in the corner for me to fix my hair and built a big bed that matches the wallpaper. He worried it wasn't very comfortable, but I said I didn't care. It's not like I can feel how uncomfortable something is.

There's a ladder in the center of the chest for me to climb out. The chest lives in the attic, so the professor wired up an old-style TV that takes a while to formulate the picture. He knows how much I like to watch the dancers in the old movies.

There's a new addition to my chest today, a bed on the other side of the room, adorned with black cushions and matching duvet. The professor has inscribed wording on the wooden headboard, but I've never been great at reading. It doesn't help that the font is in swirly writing.

The professor surprises me when his shadow encompasses the chest. He's so quiet–I never hear his footsteps.

He gently lowers the goth doll onto her bed and strokes her hair.

"This is Lisa, but you'll have to tell her that. She won't remember her name." He kneels to speak to me. It's odd when he looks into my chest like this. His face looms round and bright, the way the moon looks on TV. "I'll go into my lab to activate her. She'll be shocked, so I'll close the chest and let you ease her into it. Can you do that, Ella?"

I nod firmly; I won't let him down. The professor uses his finger to tickle underneath my chin. I can't feel the pleasurable sensation you're supposed to, but I know to laugh anyway.

The chest lid creaks when the professor closes it, leaving Lisa and me in a morbid darkness. I switch on the lamp by my bed, made from a human torch, and wait patiently on my bed for Lisa to be activated. I consider turning on the other lights, but stop when I remember the TV shows. Goths like darkness, so maybe she'll feel more at home with less light.

I run my ballet shoes through the carpet as Lisa lies still, stiff, lifeless, staring at the ceiling. The professor has painted her so she looks sad. I don't know why he did that.

My eyes widen when Lisa snaps from her upright position into a curled ball. Her jaw hangs open and she *squeals*, high-pitched and desperate, then brings her knees to her face, muffling her cries. Is…is she biting into her limbs?

Her hair covers her face, no longer straight and pristine. A bald patch winks at the back of her head – presumably, where the professor missed a stitch. His eyes aren't as good as they used to be.

"Hello?" I ask softly. Lisa lifts the hair from her eyes and peeks at me.

"Who are you?" She growls, her voice reminiscent of a TV werewolf. Husky, deep, and vicious. "You're a child!"

"I'm twelve." I cautiously step towards her. "I mean, my age is. My *name* is Ella." She flinches when I move, so I halt. "You're safe, you know."

Lisa slowly uncurls and sits hunched on the end of the bed. She scans the room suspiciously, as if trying to make sense of her new home. "Where am I?"

"A safe place." I keep my tone calm. The professor said not to tell her that she's a doll right away. That it would only cause panic. He also said she wouldn't remember anything from her human life, so try not to force any memories. "What should I call you?"

She narrows her eyes. "Lisa."

Lisa? She knew her name was Lisa? She's not supposed to remember anything from her human life. I clear my throat, even though there's nothing there. "You… you know your name is Lisa? What else do you remember?"

"What kind of stupid question is that? I'm fifteen. My best friend is Marcy, and my parents are divorced. I'll ask you *again*. Where am I?"

I can't keep my jaw from slackening. How does she know that? Did something go wrong? I raise my hands defensively. "A new home, far away from anything evil, I promise. Lisa… do you know what happened before you came here?"

She stands, unaccustomed to her new body, then stumbles and falls back onto bed, her eyebrows whooshing up. "I remember… I remember going to hospital… I had a fight with Dad…" Her eyes flutter, and she cradles her head in her hands. "Then it's black."

"Wow." I'm genuinely impressed. "I don't remember anything before…" I motion towards my body. "*This.*"

"How long have you been here?"

I shrug. The professor said he had dark hair when I first met him; but it's always been ashy to me. "My whole life."

Lisa draws her knees to her chest again and studies her hands. She bends each finger one at a time, her nostrils flaring with each squeak of her fingers. She lifts her skirt and stares at the hinges where her knees used to be, then taps her legs, the plastic loud in the silence.

She lowers her dress and gazes at the wall in front of her. Her shoulders rise and drop quickly.

"Are you okay?" I whisper, still too nervous to walk any closer.

Lisa doesn't make eye contact. "*This* is why I don't need to breathe. Or eat. Or *blink.*" She locks her jaw. "I'm a monster."

"No! No, of course not! We're *dolls!*" I smile my most encouraging smile. "*Pretty* dolls. See?" I pirouette, but she doesn't look. I don't know what else to do. Lisa has made the whole situation uncomfortable–not enjoyable like I'd imagined.

Lisa rolls on her side, her back facing me. "I'd like to be alone, please."

"Why do you want to be lonely?"

"Just because I want to be alone doesn't mean I'm lonely!" She barks.

I start to respond, but there's no point. I can't stay in this chest with her–her mood is suffocating me. If my heart worked, I'm sure my face would be flushing from frustration. I reach for the ladder in the center of the chest and climb up. I check to see whether Lisa is watching, but her head is buried in the pillow.

There's a window at the top of the ladder, so I awkwardly throw my leg through and force the remainder of my body until I topple out and land on the floor.

9

The fall doesn't hurt, but I've twisted my wrist. I try to screw it back into place, but it doesn't budge. It's hideous. My palm is just, like, staring at me, facing the wrong way.

"Ella?"

I flinch at the sound of the professor's voice. Gah. That sneaky thing again! He towers over me, but makes sure his shadow doesn't encompass me–he knows that freaks me out. He bends over and cups me in his palms, elevating me to his eyelevel.

"You jumped out of the equivalent of a three-story building after spending five minutes with Lisa?" He laughs, but it's more like a quiet wheeze. "Things didn't go so well?"

"It was awful!" I cradle my broken wrist. "*She's* awful! She's moody, rude and just, well… awful!"

With his thumb and index finger, he tweaks my wrist, putting it back into place almost immediately. "Is that better?"

I test my hand and flop it around. "Yep. Thank you! How can I stop her mood? Or is this what all teenagers are like?"

"Maybe we could help redecorate the chest?" He strokes my hair, studiously. I can't help but notice he's ignoring my last question. "We could make it feel like it's her home, too."

I lean forward to place my palm on the professor's thumb. "But she remembers her old home."

His thumb flinches, and he inhales, staring at me like I'm an alien. I don't think he's ever going to exhale. "How much of it does she remember?"

I shrug nonchalantly, but I'm unnerved by his demeanor. "Her age, her family, her friend, the hospital."

The professor splutters and puts a hand to his forehead. He almost drops me and falters to keep me from falling, then places me back on the closed chest and paces, scrunching the tips of his lab coat and scratching his head. "She's beyond repair," he mutters, before stopping to bite his nails. "She is beyond repair."

CHAPTER TWO

FIX IT

Beyond repair...

His words haunted me through the night. What had he meant? Do I really want to know?

The professor made a bed out of a half-empty tissue box so I could sleep in the attic and watch TV. He understood that I didn't want to be in the chest with Lisa.

"The recent outbreak has infected as many as ten thousand Denver residents with an over ninety-five percent fatality rate."

5:06 am. The news has been reporting the same story for hours. I flick the channel several times to try find something–*anything*–else, but the same thing is on every station. It's times like this I really wish the professor would invest in cable TV. I've seen it advertised before. They have a whole channel dedicated to musicals where people sing and dance all day, every day. A perfect paradise.

The TV's backlight is less intense now that the pale sky outside is peeking through the window. I wish we had curtains. I hate the idea of anything watching me from the outside in.

I yawn, even though I don't need to. I don't get tired if I don't sleep. I just... don't think as clearly. Memories scatter and my words jumble. I refused to sleep for three months once and by the end of the stint, I was an incoherent mess. But I didn't care. Anything was better than sleeping. Better than those vivid dreams that petrified me: images of fire and dead bodies. I haven't dreamed since I told the professor about them. Now, I can sleep peacefully in oblivious darkness.

Sleep didn't come naturally to me tonight. I kept thinking of Lisa and how she wanted to be alone, meanwhile claiming she wouldn't be lonely. That's got to be poppycock, as the professor says. Things can't work like that. Can they?

I pull the tissue over my shoulders, imagining the warmth. I like to pretend I can feel, sometimes. Even when the professor accidentally pricks his finger with something sharp... I don't know, I kind of envy him for it, even though it hurts him. It'd be nice to feel again. Anything. Something.

Lying on my side, the news anchor looking funny from the twisted angle, I rest my eyes for the first time in hours and tune out the woman's calming, melodic voice amongst the chaos.

There's pressure by my feet, like the stack of tissues beneath me has been pushed down. I open my eyes to see Lisa sitting erectly at the other end, grinning contritely. I sit up and smile politely, fighting the urge to snark. I guess I should give her another chance. We all deserve at least one.

"Hey," Lisa says, her tone a lot softer now. "I didn't mean to wake you."

"How did you get out of the chest?" I scan her body for injuries.

"Same way you did." She sweeps her hair from her eyes. "I got lonely in there."

Ah. So she *does* get lonely. "Well, that's good. I mean, it's not. But, I was getting lonely out here, so it's good you came out. Gah, I'm rambling. Sorry."

She laughs. *Wow.* I made the goth laugh! Her whole face seems to change. Her giggle is light, breezy, and completely contradictive to her fashion sense. "I had time to process everything." Her laugh fades, and her face droops. "So, I'm a doll now. I was human yesterday, and today I'm not. And you can't tell me why?"

I shake my head, uncertain how to take her new attitude. I'm not buying this sudden acceptance –it's like she has an ulterior motive or something. "The professor told me something bad happened to us as humans, so he turned us into dolls. That's all I know."

Lisa bites the inside of her mouth before forcing a smile. "I'm going to get to the bottom of this. And guess what? *You're* going to show me around. I'm sure the professor has a diary detailing his sordid workings."

"There's not much to see." I keep my voice just above a whisper. "The professor won't let us out of the attic, and I mainly spend time in the chest."

"Nah, come on!" Lisa nudges my arm with her elbow. "I'm sure there's some good stuff around here! Otherwise, what's the point of living in an *attic*? It's not World War II, you know."

"What happened in World War II?" I try, but she dismisses my question with a wave of her hand. I glance awkwardly to my ballet shoes. "Honestly, I've never left the attic. We're not allowed in the lab or downstairs."

"So there's a lab?" She speaks slowly, carefully... *suspiciously.*

"Well, yeah. The professor is, well, a *professor.* He professor-izes things in his lab." I shift uncomfortably. "Makes stuff, experiments with other stuff. In his spare time, he paints with me and teaches me things about trees."

Lisa looks like that old painting *The Scream*, although maybe a little less dramatic. "Trees?" She sounds spectacularly unimpressed.

"You study trees?"

My grin widens. Finally, the perfect chance to teach someone something! I'm sure it's more fun than learning. "Yes! Palm trees, oak trees, jacaranda trees, cotton trees, pine trees… I love trees. Trees are great! Do you like trees?"

"The word is beginning to lose all meaning." Lisa stands robotically. "I'm going to look around. Are you coming?"

I pull a displeased face, but stand and follow Lisa. We shimmy down the table leg and make our way across the room.

"It's funny." Lisa stares at her boots and scrapes them across the wooden floor. "It's not until you're this close to the ground that you realize how dirty everything is." She kicks up dust and walks through it. "Now I know why my cats were always snooty. They were disgusted by how dirty the carpets were."

I let Lisa walk the length of a human foot ahead of me to give her space. "You had cats?"

"Yep." She pauses to examine one of the abstract paintings the professor created. He never liked it, so he didn't hang it on the wall, just left it leaning against his sister's old couch. "Lovely things. Cats, I mean."

"They don't look like it on TV. In cartoons, they're always sly and evil."

Lisa walks towards the couch and picks at the stuffing coming from one of the many holes. I've always hated that couch. The hideous green isn't one of those healthy looking greens that trees have–it's sickly and covered in dust.

"Cats are anything but," Lisa's voice drops to a whisper. "They're full of personality. They're loving and caring. Things are never what they appear to be; especially humans. Sometimes you get flashes of the 'real' person, and we're stupid enough to mistake the 'real them' for being 'out of character'. The person we never see is who they really are."

"So who are you, then?" I join Lisa in picking at the stuffing.

"Are you the grumpy goth or are you the chatty explorative?"

She looks at me in silence for a while, her face neutral. "Neither." She turns on her heel and walks beneath the coffee table, piled high with old newspapers. I've never bothered to read them. What's done is done, if you want my opinion.

"Who knows who I am, anymore." She jumps over the vacuum cord, landing a bit wobbly. The vacuum is always out, ready to clean, but the professor never gets around to it. I was a perfectionist years ago. I used to yell at him for not vacuuming or cleaning well enough, so he just stopped doing it. After a while, I just got used to the mess. "We've been conditioned to forget, for some reason. Yet we're made up of memories—so what are we without them?"

"But you remember your human life, don't you?" I leap over the cord and jog to catch up to Lisa. She walks deceptively fast, despite her unsteadiness.

"Some of it." She sighs, her upturned eyes making me feel sorry for her. "The things I remember, I wish were forgotten. It makes me wonder about the things I *have* forgotten. Are they good or are they even worse than the memories I've kept?"

She stops in her tracks and points at the locked door. I never noticed the peeled paint around the edges. Maybe it's because Lisa has been so judgmental about her surroundings. To be honest, all of a sudden, I'm more than a little embarrassed by the state of the attic.

"That. Is that the lab?"

"Yeah." I tent my fingers together. "But we can't go in."

"Of course, we can."

"No, I mean we physically can't. The professor has the key. Plus, look how high the doorknob is. We'd never reach."

Lisa's gaze drops to the floor. She looks sad, or disappointed, but I struggle distinguishing. Squeaking up, she places her hands against the door as if to test its strength. She lightly kicks at it before taking a step back to observe its reaction. Suddenly, she shrugs and flashes a smile. "There's a way in. I'll work it out. When I do, I'm going to turn us back into humans. Then, we'll *lock up* that professor. He can rot in a cell for what he did to us!"

I make a strange sound somewhere in between a gasp and a scoff. "Why would we lock him up? He didn't do anything wrong. He *saved* us."

Lisa narrows her eyes. "That's what he's brainwashed you into believing. Look around, Ella. You're in a prison."

I don't break eye contact with her. I don't want her thinking I'm easily manipulated, so I remain still, fighting the urge to check out my alleged prison. When I refuse to blink, she smiles—looking almost proud—then flicks her hair, frowning when it doesn't flow smoothly over her shoulder. That's one of the bad things about our wigs—they're wiry.

"Oh well," she says calmly. *Too* calmly. I'm admittedly not bright, but I know she's masking whatever resentment that's boiling up now. "I'm sure there are other things you can show me."

For some bizarre reason, I panic. I've never had to entertain anyone before. There's pressure on me to amuse her now. I don't feel pressured when I watch TV or dance on my own. Man, I never would've guessed company would be so *stressful*.

"*Well*," I elongate the word to buy time. "We could discuss trees?"

Lisa's arms squeak when she crosses them. "Ella, are you honestly telling me you don't do anything up here?"

"I do things," I say defensively. "They're just things you wouldn't be interested in. You can look around some more, but there's nothing here. Just junk. Empty boxes, half-painted canvases, old skis…"

"Did you used to ski?"

Seriously? I raise my hands and speak apologetically. "Lisa, I don't remember. You know that."

She sweeps her fringe from her eyes. "Oh." There's no tone in her voice. She merely turns away and walks into the attic's darkest corner.

"Lisa, wait!" I follow her into the darkness. I don't like the dark. What if we never come out?

"Darkness calls when the sunlight falls, hi-ho, hi-ho," she chants eerily until we hit a dead-end.

"There's nothing here," I say in the direction of her outline. "Let's go back to the chest. Maybe we could watch TV together?"

"That's boring. We're leaving the attic."

I shake my head, even though she can't see me in the darkness. "No, Lisa. I don't want to leave."

"Oh come on," she says, her tone facetious. "Think of it as an adventure."

I hesitate. I do enjoy the concept of adventures. I mean, a few times a week I play *Ella's Rescue Squad* on my tape recorder, but that's just acting. "Can I come with you and, you know, come back afterwards?"

Lisa's silhouette shrugs. "I don't care what you do. You can either follow me through this crevasse or you can stand here like a loser."

"I'm not a loser…" I say softly, but Lisa has already ducked her head and walked through the crooked gap.

I tent my fingers nervously, ignoring the screams in my head that urge me not to follow. Slowly, I bend over and squeeze through the hole. I didn't think it was possible for it to get any darker, but somehow, the black overlays the black.

"Lisa?" I whisper, jolting when I run into a roadblock. I wave my hands to the side and find myself at a crossroad. "Lisa, are you still here? Which way did you turn?"

No response.

"Lisa?" I blindly bounce off the walls when I turn to the left.

There's a giggle in the distance. It's ominous and unsettling, but I stumble towards it. I see light up ahead and frantically run towards it, the hysteria bubbling inside of me.

I emerge to find Lisa standing underneath a desk with her arms folded. She smirks and shakes her head. "You're one paranoid dolly."

I don't respond. I'm too distracted by my foot sinking into the white floor. I wave my hands above my head. "Lisa, help! The floor is eating me! It's up to my ankle!"

"Ella." Lisa rolls her eyes. She turns on her heel and wraps her limbs around the table leg like a koala, inching up until she stands proudly on the surface. "It's just carpet, stupid."

Carpet? I lift my foot from the floor and lower it again, watching my ballet slipper disappear into the fluff. I've never walked in proper carpet before. I study the rest of the room and am surprised by how bright it is. The attic is so dirty and dingy—it's the polar opposite of what I'm guessing is the professor's bedroom. The walls are mauve and match the bedspread. A portrait of an older woman, in her fifties maybe, hangs above the professor's desk. She's smiling, but her eyes are heavy and full of sorrow.

"Huh…" Lisa's grunt startles me. "Hey, Ella? This looks like lab notes or a diary, or something. Get up here, I can't make out his scribble."

"Then maybe we shouldn't read it?" I carefully make my way up the table leg. When I reach the top, the *neatness* takes me aback. The surface is white, like the carpet, and only an empty mug and pen are on the table. Why doesn't he keep the attic this tidy?

Lisa sits on the diary cross-legged, her eyes scanning the contents. "How many dolls have come before me?"

I shrug. "The professor said there have been several before me. They come and go, but I've never met them."

"Where do you think they go?"

I let loose another shrug. I've never really thought about it before.

"He's talking about me in his diary." Lisa points out her name. "See? I think it says: *I'm activating Lisa today.* It's hard to read. What do you see?"

I tilt my head to the side to try and make out his writing. It doesn't help that Lisa stares at me as if I'm about to decipher all the mysteries in the world. "Lisa, I lost the ability to read when my memories were wiped."

She digs her nails into the page and glares at me. "What use are you then?" Her head jerks when she looks at the diary again. "Pathetic doll."

I'm glad the professor walks in before I can respond, because I have no idea what to say. He does most of the speaking—well, more spluttering really—anyway.

"How did you girls get in here?"

"Through the mouse hole." I point at the tiny gap in the wall.

"Shut up, Ella!" Lisa barks, tripping on her own hair when she tries to stand. "Professor, it's none of your business. Tell me why I'm a doll! Turn me back!"

"I can't do that." He scoops us both into his lab coat pockets, then walks out so fast, I feel like I'm on a plane. Or rather, what I imagine being on a plane would feel like. We go through two doors to reach the attic, and he places us back in the treasure chest. "Thank you *very* much, Lisa. I have a busy day today, and now I have to spend it plastering over the holes to keep you from getting out."

"You speak as if I'm a rodent," Lisa hisses, folding her arms and turning away. "Plaster the whole room. I *dare* you. I'll still find a way out of here."

I glance at her, stunned by her rudeness, then at the professor, unsurprised by the tightness in his face. I feel like reminding him to breathe. He goes to say something, but thinks better of it and turns on his heel. I grimace when he slams the door, certain that it's close to coming off its hinges.

"That was awkward," I say to Lisa who doesn't smile even when I nudge her playfully. "We'll never do that again, okay?"

Lisa doesn't reply.

"Do you want to come and watch TV with me?"

She stares at me and twists her face. "No."

She climbs out of the chest and walks towards the dark corner of the attic, her hands tucked between her underarms.

Well, fine. She can stay there. If she's going to be a black hole of misery that absorbs my happiness, then she belongs in the shadows!

I feel bad for thinking that once I climb out of the chest. As I turn on the TV and dive into my tissue-box bed, a strong feeling overwhelms me: this will be the first of many nights that will be spent alone.

I don't know how long Lisa has been standing there. I only just woke up. She's gripping a pair of scissors in one hand, the handle resting on the floor, the scissors standing almost as tall as her. She lets go of the scissors, and they clatter to the floor.

"Lisa?" My voice goes pathetically meek. "You're creeping me out. What are you doing?"

The moonlight glints off the scissors, contrasting Lisa's body, which looks more like a shadow in the inky night.

She slips her boot through one of the holes in the scissors and bends over so that her enviably long hair dangles against the tip.

"Lisa! Lisa, don't be stupid. Your hair won't grow back!"

"Good." Her voice is husky again; it's like a demon is wedged inside her throat. She snips the right side of her hair and in an instant, it detaches and falls to the ground. That's so disappointing—her hair was lovely. She snips it again, evening the other side out so that she has a short bob. "He made me how he wanted me to be. I'm not his doll!"

Lisa stands, flicking her new hair. She smiles, as though a huge weight has been lifted off her shoulders.

She walks purposefully to the other side of the table where there's a tub of pens and brushes and old pots of paint. She heaves a brush from the tub and awkwardly maneuvers it into one of the colors, but I can't make out which one in the dark. She shifts the paintbrush so that it's pointed at her face. Before I have time to object, she presses her eye into the tip. "I don't have blue eyes!" She shrieks, blinding herself further when she pushes her other eye into the brush. "He made me have blue eyes! They're *not mine*! *THEY'RE NOT MINE!*"

I pull the tissue over my head and curl into a ball, covering my ears, desperate to block her out. I don't understand why her moods leap from happy to crazy in an instant—it's, well yeah, it's crazy. Maybe if I get lost in my own thoughts, she'll disappear. I'll think of birds… and butterflies… and the calming ocean tides.

"*MY BRAIN IS SCATTERED, MY HEART IS BATTERED!*" Lisa cries, popping open the lid to a pot of paint.

Birds…

Butterflies…

Calming ocean tides…

CHAPTER THREE

WHISPERS

What do you mean you've *lost* her?" The professor has never raised his voice before. Not to me, anyway.

"Well, I've been sleeping in the tissue box all week, haven't I? Haven't been in my room for days! She's around somewhere, I'm sure. She can't go far…"

The professor rubs his cheeks and mouth. He hasn't shaved in days, and it only makes him look disheveled. "True. She would only be in this room. When was the last time you saw her?"

I shrug. It's Wednesday, and I'm due for a new leotard. I'm sick of orange. "Five days ago, maybe. She cut her hair."

"What!"

"Yeah. To about here." I raise my hand to my chin. "And she found one of your old paintbrushes and tattooed her arms. She looked ridiculous trying to use that thing; it was as big as her. The tattoos are just squiggly and messy. Like all tattoos, I suppose."

The professor picks me up from the table and tightens his grip, which makes me feel like I could break at any minute. "Show me where she was."

"Professor, please, your hand. I don't like it."

"Show me where you last saw her!"

"Professor," I squeak, trying to wriggle from his grip, but I'm stuck. A burning pulse wraps around my waist the more he squeezes. "Please let go!"

"Ella!"

Salty tears don't run down my cheeks like in the movies, but I let out pained moans and howl. I think... I think this is what crying is.

The professor is shocked. He lowers me to the table, kisses my head, and tickles my chin, but it doesn't stop me from crying. I wrap my arms around my waist, the pain from his grip throbbing.

"Why are you crying?" His tone is softer now.

"It hurts," I say between sobs. "It hurts so much!"

"What hurts? You're a doll! You're not supposed to hurt!"

I point at my sides, certain that this is what bruising must be. "I know!" Wait a minute. It hurts. I'm actually feeling something! I smile through the pain. "Wow. I can *feel*! Ouch."

"Not for years..." The professor's voice is almost a whisper. He sighs. "Everything's gone wrong since I activated Lisa. Sianne warned me about the experiment. I'm just an obsessed, old man."

"Who's Sianne?"

"No one." He clears his throat. "Are you still hurting?"

"Yes, but it's bearable now."

The professor scratches at his stubble. "Good, good." He begins to say something, but changes his mind. "Well, um, I should get ready for Gabby. You'll keep an eye out for Lisa?"

I nod. "I will. Gabby's your granddaughter, right?"

"Yes, and she will be here soon. You know, I introduced you to Lisa in the hopes that you could finally have a friend other than me," the professor trails off, staring at me like a crazed animal. "Maybe Gabby will be your friend."

I must've misheard him. "Sorry?"

"Gabby. She's your age, you know. I mean, a year younger, but I think you'll really like one another."

I struggle to form words. "But, she's human, right?"

The professor picks me up, cradling me gently in his hands. He walks towards the chest and opens it, lowering me onto my bed. "Yes. Just like you were."

"But you always said humans wouldn't understand talking dolls! That's why you keep me up here!"

"I think Gabby might be an exception. She's good at keeping secrets. It's time you had someone else to talk to besides me."

"But…" I don't get a chance to respond before he kisses my head, switches my lamp on, and closes the chest.

I don't know how I feel about meeting another human. It's one thing to watch them on TV, but to interact with them is kinda daunting. I'm more worried about how she will feel about me–the professor said it's not exactly common for dolls to be alive. The TV seems to support this notion.

Gah, I'm overthinking. My mind feels jumbled after crying, like it's not working right or something. I must be tired.

It feels nice to be back in my bedroom after being forced into the tissue-box bed for a full week. I snuggle into the covers and stretch out as far as I can. I've never appreciated the comforting glow of the lamp before, or the butterfly stickers on the walls.

I'm home.

I'm lost. A long road stretches out beyond what I can see. I'm cold, but I don't move. I just sit in the middle of it, unable to see beyond my own hand in the darkness.

There's no moon, no stars, no life. The only sound is my heart pounding in my ears.

I'm wet, but not from water. The substance is sticky and thick. I'm dying.

"Ella!"

It takes a while for me to snap out of the dream. I almost don't recognize Lisa now that she has such short hair. She didn't do a great job cutting it. It's jagged, and somehow makes her look older.

"Where have you been?" I whisper as if it's the dead of night.

"Hiding," Lisa whispers in return, darting her eyes around the chest. "Ella, do dolls feel things?"

"Like confusion and frustration? Yeah."

"No!" she snaps. "Do you feel pain or warmth?"

I pause, uncertain as to how I should respond. "We're not supposed to."

"But do you?"

"I did today." I meet Lisa's manic gaze. "What did you do? Where have you been?"

Lisa studies the floor and bites her nails, which have been messily splattered with purple paint. Crazed with excitement, her eyes are no longer aqua like mine. She's painted them violet, covering the white sparkle and shrinking her once big pupils. She doesn't look like me anymore. "I got into the lab!"

"*How?*" I struggle to keep my voice low.

"Dilapidated place like this is bound to have a maze of mouse holes. I've been experimenting in there," she mutters.

"Experimenting with what?"

"Broken dolls."

She smirks at me as she pulls herself up the ladder and out of the chest. I don't ask where she's going. I can only hope she doesn't come back.

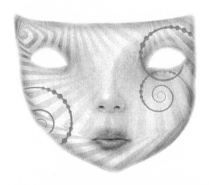

CHAPTER FOUR

GABBY

This week, on *Ella Rescue Squad*: our petite hero protects her love interest, Andy, by thwarting the great and powerful ghost, Ruze-go-moto!" I pretend to be the audience listening to the radio show and cheer and clap for myself. "Will she win? Will she lose? Stay tuned to find out!"

I hit the pause button on the recorder. I found it a couple of years ago, and the professor said I could use it to diarize. It's dusty, and the tape inside looks worn and tired, but it's a fun way to pass the time. It's the size of a brick and the keys are sticky, so I have to push the record and rewind button extra hard.

Suddenly, I realize something. I record imagination time a few times a week, but I used to speak about my thoughts–thoughts I don't think I have anymore. I want to know if I used to be as pessimistic and cynical as Lisa.

Ella Rescue Squad can wait for now. I go towards a pile of old tapes and find the first one I ever used. It's not heavy to carry, it's just awkward. When I put it in the recorder, I press rewind, and the wheels spin until they hit the beginning of the tape. It plays automatically, and all it produces at first is static and crackling. I sit down and pull my legs to my chest, keen to hear its content for the first time. I've never listened before. Often the professor will just give me a new tape or I record over the old ones.

"What's it do?" My voice says through the speaker. I laugh and shield my face in embarrassment. I. Sound. Horrendous.

"It's a tape recorder," the professor explains tenderly. "It... records. It's doing it now. Say hello!"

"Hello!" my awful voice says.

"Now I'm going to leave you with it as I have an appointment," the professor says, his voice getting harder to hear. "Press this button to stop, okay?"

"Okay!" I reply in unison with myself, remembering the first time the professor left me with this old clunker. The door closes in the distance, and the old me clears her throat.

"I don't really know what I'm supposed to say," my voice on the recorder mumbles nervously. "I'm not happy, I suppose. The nightmares are getting worse—the one with the fire. I'm..." The old-me sighs and pauses. "I'm miserable."

The recording stops there. I blink. I don't remember saying that! I go to stand and fast-forward the silence, but my voice comes through again.

"I've never gone this far." It sounds scared, but it's just my terrible acting. I remember this imagination time. "Felicity, my human friend, has stowed me away and is taking me to...*the school library*. I'm not sure how I'll fair with all the other kids! They're so big and I'm so small, but luckily I've got my furry friend, Jack the Dog, to help me out!"

I roll my eyes and press stop. Why don't I have any recollection of the rest of that first entry? And how soon afterwards did I record my next one, because I seem as chipper as a squirrel that just found his nuts?

The professor knocks on the door before entering, probably conscious of the time he walked in on my last imagination time and ruined it. I was so annoyed–I was just about to slay a dragon, and he barged in asking me what tie he should wear.

"You can come in." I fold my arms, frowning at the recorder.

He enters with a cartoonish smile and motions towards the shoebox he's holding. "I've got some clothes for you to choose from!" His face glows. "I'm so excited for you to meet my granddaughter. You'll love each other!"

I reciprocate his happy expression. I can worry about the recorder later.

"She's sitting downstairs at the moment." He's unable to contain his grin. "I told her I have a big surprise for her, but she has no idea that it's you! We better hurry." He rummages through the box. "What about the golden tutu?"

"No, no, it's too much like the orange I've been wearing." I wave it away, and the professor pulls another from the shoebox, holding it between his finger and thumb.

"What about purple?"

I shudder. It's too much like Lisa's eyes and fingernails. Lisa has officially ruined purple for me.

"I'm kind of over purple," I say politely. "I was wondering if you have a dress instead of a tutu? I thought because I'm meeting Gabby, I should look my best." I twirl towards the tissue-box and bounce on the padding.

The professor's shoulders roll back when he readjusts his glasses. "But you're a dancer."

"I know, but being a dancer doesn't mean I *always* have to wear leotards and tutus. Maybe it'd be nice to change it up a bit?"

The professor scoffs and dangles a pink leotard above my head, motioning for me to take it. "Don't be silly, Ella. Put this on, and I'll get Gabby."

"Fine." I sigh.

The professor grins and leaves the attic. I pull down the straps of my leotard, wriggle out of it and squeeze into its pink counterpart.

It's a bit tighter. I mean, it's not uncomfortable, but it looks funny. I have a huge wedgie that the tutu won't hide. Great–that's going to make a swell first impression. *Look, I'm a dancing doll ignorant to the bum cheeks hanging out back.* Just *great.*

The door squeaks, and the professor enters. There's a child behind him, too difficult to make out from my angle. I perch down on the table edge, swinging my legs anxiously as the professor and Gabby walk closer.

Wait. It's not ladylike to swing your legs, is it? I immediately cross them and place my hands in my lap. Gosh, I'm nervous. I'm meeting another human, and it feels way too surreal. I mean, this human is *real.* Not like the Felicity-human I made up in imagination time.

"Gabby?" The professor speaks to his granddaughter the way he speaks to me. "I'd like you to meet someone."

He steps to the side and leads Gabby towards the table.

My mouth drops when I see her. She's breathtakingly beautiful–you know, if I *could* breathe. Her hair is thick, crimped, and worn well below her shoulders. Her lips turn up even when she isn't smiling, so her face always looks pleasant and welcoming. She's pale, but I don't think it's from the lack of sunlight. Her eyes are heavy and dark, like she's fighting the onset of a cold.

Oh my God. She's looking at me. I instinctively don't move; I just watch her in awe. Breathing and blinking come so naturally to her–she probably doesn't even know she's doing it.

I love her dress. It has blue and white stripes at the top, with navy at the bottom–kind of like a sailor. I glance at my humiliatingly tight leotard and cringe. Why couldn't I look nice, like her?

"She's pretty!" Gabby hurries up to me. "Is this the doll you said you were painting?"

I refrain from smiling. *She said I was pretty!* She leans over and rests her chin on the table, tapping my legs with her finger.

"It is. Her name is Ella."

"Can I pick her up?"

"Not just yet," the professor says, cautiously stepping closer. "Ella is a very special doll."

Gabby's eyes widen, and she stands. "Really? Why?"

Here it comes. The moment of truth. I really hope Gabby takes the news well. It'd be awesome to be friends with a human girl and not some psychotic goth doll.

The professor winks at me, encouraging me to move.

I smile at Gabby first, not wanting to shock her. She gasps and returns to her position with her chin on the table to view me better. "Cool! A robot!"

I uncross my legs and stand to curtsey. "Not quite, Gabby."

"She talks, too! Wow!" She bounces on her heels, squealing with excitement. "Is she mine?"

"Ella is a real little girl, Gabby." The professor squeezes Gabby's shoulder with his hand. "She used to be like you, many years ago. Something happened, so I made her into a doll."

"You can do that?" There is skepticism in Gabby's voice, but she masks it with a giggle. She offers her finger to me, so I gracefully shake it.

"You're not freaked out?" I ask quietly, too nervous for anything louder than a whisper.

Gabby shakes her head. "No way. Come on, let's play! Have you ever been down the slide?"

I feel betrayed for some reason. The window up here only allows me to see the side of the house and part of the road, so I didn't even know we had a slide. Why hasn't the professor ever taken me there? "I've never left the attic," I say, unable to maintain eye contact.

"Oh." She shifts uncomfortably. "Well, there's a first for everything! How about I take you?"

I nod and leap into Gabby's palms, who laughs when I lightly scratch at her skin, trying to tickle her the way the professor tickles me.

"This is so weird!" Gabby chuckles, bringing me closer to nuzzle into me.

"Um, actually, no, we're not going to do that," the professor lifts me from Gabby's hands and puts me back on the table. "You two can play here today."

"Here? It's so dusty and dark! Let's just go outside!" Gabby demands eagerly, not tearing her gaze from me.

The professor stands taller, his jaw locked and his muscles tensed. "No." His word is firm, vicious, final. He doesn't say goodbye when he pulls the door behind him. It doesn't slam, per se–the professor's far too soft for that–but closes with just enough force for us to know that he's mad.

Gabby points at her head and twirls her index finger in one direction. "Grandpa is crazy. A real control freak. But he's boring. So tell me about you! What'd you like to do? I'm up for anything!"

I hesitate. That slide sure sounded good. "There's not much to tell. What about you? Do you go to school? What food do you eat? What's swimming like? Have you kissed a boy?"

Gabby throws her head back when she laughs, and small creases form beneath her eyes. "I'm only eleven! I had a boyfriend, but we only held hands, which was weird enough! You've never done any of those things?"

"Maybe…" I bite my lip, plastic against plastic. "If I did, I sure can't remember."

"Well, that's horrible." Gabby scans the room and strides towards the corner where the abandoned canvases and paint are.

"What are you doing?" I shimmy down from the table to follow her.

She picks up a blank canvas and kneels. "We're going t–" She looks at the table, a worried expression crossing her face. "Where'd you go?"

I laugh and wave my arms wildly. "Down here."

Gabby spots me and sighs. "Phew! Thought I lost you already! Okay, we're going to make a bucket list!"

"A bucket list?" It's a long walk for me to reach her, but when I do, I climb into her lap to see the canvas from her perspective. "What's a bucket list?"

"Oh my God, you're so cute!" she coos, stroking my hair. "Oh… darn, I'm so sorry. I have to remind myself you're not a doll. You're just like me, and I probably wouldn't like someone petting my head all the time. Focus, Gabby, focus. Anyway, a *bucket list* is a list of all the things you want to do in your life before you, erm, kick the bucket. Start listing, Ella!"

"You wouldn't like someone stroking your head all the time?" The professor always does it to me.

Gabby sticks her tongue out. "No way. It's… now, what's that word Dad used the other day? Condensing? No, condescending, maybe? Yeah, that's it. It'd be *condescending* if someone kept petting your head like an animal's. Am I using the right term?"

I readjust the ribbons on my ballet shoes, ensuring that the knot isn't visible. "Yeah," I push out quietly past a sudden tightness in my throat. "That's the perfect word."

"Cool. I'm trying to work on my vocabulary. Mom's an author, so she wants to make sure I speak well. So many of my friends say things like 'brung' instead of 'brought', and it drives her insane. We're off topic! First bucket list item?"

My mind flickers to a documentary on sharks I saw the other day. The water looked so refreshing. And oh, to be able to defy gravity! Swimming seemed like the closest thing to flying. "I want to go to the ocean." I slam a palm against my lips. Did I really just say that?

"Great!" Gabby dabs the paintbrush in the used water the professor never cleaned out. She writes OCEAN in bold, blue letters followed by a fish. She's not a bad artist. "What next? Mine is to put syrup on spaghetti!"

I laugh, even though I don't really understand the context. I don't know how outrageous it must be because I can't remember tasting food.

"What now? You're a dancer, so I bet you'd like to dance on a real stage?"

I nod viciously, vivid images of me onstage exploding in my mind. "That would amazing! I'd also like to pet a dog, or a cat. I'm suspicious of cats, but I'll give them a go anyway."

Gabby paints the face of a dog and a cat, their whiskers entwining around one another. "I'm going to say hug a lion cub. Or koala. Or seal! Heck, hug any wild animal. Your turn."

I glance at the window outside and think longingly of hearing the birds chirp in the fresh air and not through a muffled dusty pane. "I want to go outside." I feel almost disobedient for even suggesting it, but I don't understand why I'm not allowed the freedom of my own backyard. The professor says he's scared that I'll break outside, but I don't see how.

Gabby beams and lowers the canvas to the floor, then lifts me as she stands and gently puts me in her dress pocket.

"What are you doing?" I shriek. "Are you stealing me?"

"There's no time like the present." Gabby uses one of the tissues to wipe the dust from the window. Instantly, the attic brightens. The daylight is so much more vibrant than I realized. I always thought they exaggerated it on TV, but I was wrong. It turns out TV couldn't even encompass just how beautiful it really is outside.

"That's better already, isn't it?" Gabby unlatches the lock and shoves at the window, the glass rattling when she pulls on it. "Wow, this is really stuck."

"What are you doing?" I squirm to get out of her pocket, but it's deceptively deep. I fumble and fall only deeper, fighting through the fabric to poke my head through the gap.

"I'm taking you outside."

"You're going to throw me outside?" I gasp, more than just a hint of hysteria in my voice.

"No, silly," Gabby says calmly, pushing her weight against the window. "*We're* going outside, and then *you* are trying the slide."

"But why do we have to climb through the window?"

"Because I *bet* Grandpa's in his study, writing in his diary or playing Sudoku or chess. It's how he winds down. He'll be there for an hour at least, but probably two considering how miffed he was. If we go down the stairs, he'll hear us and freak out. We'll sneak through the window, down the drainpipe, and we'll be back before he even knows we left. I'm a good climber, so I promise we'll be fine. Deal?"

The window gives, and Gabby slides it open, albeit jerky and noisy.

I don't know. I've never done anything I wasn't supposed to, no matter how much I wanted to. Rules are there for a reason; they shouldn't be questioned, and they definitely shouldn't be broken.

"Deal," I say, my voice high and breathy.

Gabby's movements are rocky and being in her dress is probably what it's like to be in a boat during a storm. I clutch onto the edge of her pocket to see what's happening, but a lot of it is a blur.

She dangles one leg through the window first, the same way I climb out of the treasure chest. The other leg follows, before she inches her bottom closer to the edge.

I'm terrified–for a lot of reasons. Not just because I'll get in trouble for going outside, but I'm petrified that Gabby will fall.

She waves her foot by the drainpipe, hitting it to test its strength. She reaches with her hands and hugs it like a koala cuddling a tree. I can't even appreciate the outside world–all I can do is watch Gabby's scrunched-up face. The wind blows, and whips her hair around her, and ruffles her dress, and it's enough for me to feel like I'm being thrashed around by a hurricane.

"This is hard in a dress," she says, her voice tight.

I don't reply–she doesn't need the distraction.

The drainpipe shakes, barely holding Gabby's weight.

"Uh-oh," she says.

"Let's go back!" I yell, sickened by how far away the ground is. I've never dangled so high above anything. What if I break completely? If Gabby lands on me, that might be it. I might be beyond repair–just like Lisa.

"No, it's okay," Gabby says, perpetually optimistic. She loosens her grip and slides halfway down like firefighters do on those poles in the movies. We're not far from the bottom, maybe a few human feet, but it might as well be a mile. "This might shock you a bit. Hold on, Ella."

Without giving me a second to process her words, she releases her grip and falls.

I can't help screaming as the ground streams towards me. The force of the hit rattles me, but we're okay. Gabby crouches, steadying herself before she stands.

"Phew!" she squeals. "Lucky you were weighing my dress down! It nearly went up over my head! That would've been embarrassing!"

"Out of everything that just happened, *that's* what bothered you the most?"

Gabby laughs, dusting herself off. She pushes on a gate that squeaks when it moves, kind of like I do when I stretch my legs.

We're in the backyard. We're *actually* in the backyard. Gabby heads towards swings and slide that are next to a sandpit. Wow. There are so many things out here to play on, and I had no idea they even existed.

It's a little scary outside, but only because it's a new experience. It's a lot more vibrant than I could've ever imagined. The flowers are in bloom, and the grass looks so soft, I'd give anything to feel it against my skin. The sky is grey though–I can't find the sun or see a patch of blue.

Our backyard looks like most of the ones on TV. Not particularly big and surrounded by other houses that look similar to ours. We have a brown fence that boxes us in with a tree that the professor hasn't educated me on situated in the corner. It's tall, and its trunk doesn't sprout branches until the very tip, where it morphs into a baldish Christmas tree. I can't believe I don't know what it is. I'll have to find a way to query the professor.

"Time to cross one thing off the bucket list!" She rushes to the ladder, not accustomed to a living doll crouching in her pocket. She must keep forgetting I'm there because I'm starting to feel sick. Do dolls get sick?

She watches her footing as she climbs and sits at the top. It's taken her no time at all. For me, it would've taken forever.

"Nervous?" She pulls me from her pocket and places me between her legs.

"Very." The slide is long–too long–and I'm regretting wanting this in the first place. I look up, my neck creaking. "I can't do this, Gabby. Let's go back to the attic."

"OH MY GOD, you're so cute!" she squeals. "I promise, this is *fun*."

"But I'm worried I'll go too far and break."

"You won't break. I've pushed a lot of my dolls down the slide before. They got a little dirty, but they never broke."

I try to compose my thoughts, but I feel lightheaded. It's like when I dream–nothing pieces together right, and my thoughts are unclear. I suppose this is what nerves and adrenalin must be like.

"I'm going to push you." Gabby nudges my back. "It'll be over before you know it, and you'll be begging to go again. Ready?"

"No."

"Ready?"

"*No.*"

"GO!" I don't feel her push me, but the grass rushes towards me just like it did when Gabby dropped from the drainpipe. I scream in preparation for my body's destruction and draw my knees to my chest, deafened by the susurration of my ballet slippers scraping against the steel.

I slow down as I reach the end of the slide, only centimeters from the edge. I remain still, a little dazed by the experience.

Gabby whooshes down behind me, beaming. "What did you think, huh? Fun, right?"

I raise my eyebrows at her and smile. "I didn't break!"

"Of course, you didn't! You're not as delicate as you think! What next?"

I glance at the swing that sways in the breeze. "That thing?"

Gabby's nose scrunches when she shakes her head. "That's the best one, so let's save that for last. Jump in my pocket, and I'll take you across the monkey bars."

There's a rumble in the distance, and Gabby stops mid-reach. "Damn it. It's going to storm. We better do this, then hurry back in. I'll take you on the swing next time, promise!"

I raise my arms so Gabby can grip my waist and slip me into her pocket. She jogs towards the monkey bars and climbs the ladder.

I crouch in her pocket, fighting the voice in my head that urges me to stop. "Gabby? Can we not do this?"

"What are you talking about?" She reaches for the first bar. Her body tugs when her feet drop from the step and her arms tremble, holding her bodyweight.

"Gabby, I really don't want to do this!"

She swings to the next bar and I shield my eyes, holding back strained whimpers.

"Gabby!" I shriek. "Let me out!"

"Chill, Ella! I got this!" She swings to the next bar, faltering. She regains her grip, reaches for the next bar... and slips, her body mere moments away from crashing into the ground.

It's like I'm not in her pocket anymore. I'm the one swinging, losing control, and slipping. I fall flat on my back, my head smacking into the grass so hard, I see a flash of white. I land on my arm, and the waves of pain rush through my broken joint. I can feel the twist, the break, swelling beneath my back. My throat hurts from screaming, but I don't care. It's the only way to get the pain out...

"Ella? Ella? Stop! Ella, stop! Please, stop!"

"But I've broken my arm!"

Gabby's face appears, but I'm still screaming and nursing my arm. She has placed me on the grass and is on all fours, fanning me.

I must look more coherent once I stop screaming, because Gabby sighs in relief. Wait. Why is she wet? I glance up and see droplets of rain plummet to earth. I hate the rain. It's like the sky is crying. It makes Gabby look a lot younger now that her hair sticks to her face.

"What happened?" I ask, the pain subsiding.

"I missed the bar and dropped, like, a foot. Then you started screaming hysterically!"

"So I *didn't* fall and break my arm?"

"No. It was like you had some Vietnam flashback. Did you fall off the monkey bars when you were a human?"

I pause. "I'm not sure…" Maybe I did. That daydream was way too vivid.

The rain is loud and heavy, but nothing is louder than the back door slamming against the bricks.

"*ELLA!*" The professor stands at the doorway, his expression beyond mortified. Running comes unnaturally to him, his limbs flailing uncontrollably as he slides to his knees and pushes Gabby out of the way. "Ella! You're filthy! You were screaming! Are you broken?"

"No," I say softly, but he interrupts me by scooping me into his arms.

"Go to your father's old room, Gabrielle!" On the verge of yelling and despite the throbbing vein in his forehead, he manages to maintain his composure. "I can't believe what you've just done!"

"We needed to have fun!" Gabby wipes the mud from her wrists, thoroughly unrepentant. "She lives in that attic all day and night. How is that a life, Grandpa? I don't care about repossessions anymore!"

"*Repercussions,*" the professor corrects through gritted teeth. "You should *always* care about repercussions!"

"Screw repercussions!" Gabby shrieks, storming through the back door.

I cuddle into the professor, who unbuttons his jacket so that I can hide from the rain.

He takes me upstairs and back into the safety of the attic. He spots the open window and hisses, rushing towards it and bolting it tight. He puts me on the table and pulls up a chair so that he can be eyelevel with me.

"You're drenched," he says remorsefully, running his fingers through my hair, which now hangs below my shoulders. "I'll have to get a new wig. You'll never be able to put it up in a bun like this."

"It's okay," I whisper. "Really. Gabby didn't kidnap me or anything. I wanted to go outside."

"You can't go outside!" He stretches over me to grab a tissue to dab at my limbs. "See what happens when you go outside?"

"It was fun," I say defensively, although I don't understand why I had such an intense daydream.

"Were you hurting again? Is that why you were screaming?"

"No. I was just... scared." I also really, really suck at lying. This conversation needs to go somewhere else, fast. "Have you seen Lisa?"

"No." He dries my hair next. "Have you?"

"No." Two consecutive lies. If there is a doll Hell, I'd be in it.

"That's a worry..." His voice trails off, and he stops drying my hair, then shakes his head and continues. "You've had enough excitement for one day. How about you get settled in the chest, and I'll lay out new clothes for you?"

"Could I please have a dress like Gabby?" I clap my hands into a begging position.

The professor's expression is unsettling. It's like he's hurt and trying to cover it with a very unconvincing smile. "I only have tutus and leotards for you. That's what you wanted."

"But can't I have–"

"No." We remain in silence for several seconds. He kicks back the chair and kisses my head, leaving me in the solitude that is loneliness.

My only company is the gentle patter of rain and the roar of thunder. A fitting metaphor. I feel like I'm the sky tears, trying to escape the overbearing nature. It's only when I cower behind the stool leg as the lightning flashes that I realize that the professor, perhaps, isn't the thunder or lightning in my metaphor. He's something much worse.

He's the eye of the storm.

CHAPTER FIVE

CHUCKY

The storm intensifies. Sticks and other small pieces keep flinging against the window. It's really creeping me out. I keep imagining a demonic deer hovering outside, saliva dripping from its snarl as it headbutts the pane.

Why a demonic deer? No clue. Deer are terrifying. I've never even been able to finish *Bambi*. Most people are traumatized by the mother dying, whereas the fact that the story revolves around deer is what gives me the creeps.

My bed isn't as comforting as usual. It's the one place I always felt safe in, but not tonight. I keep kicking the sheets off, frustrated by the permanent point in my feet. I want to flex and stretch them out and experience what it's like to walk flatfooted. Just because I like dancing doesn't mean my *whole life* should be doing that. The professor won't even sew me pajamas–the clothes he laid out was just another red tutu. Sequined, no less. How's that supposed to lure me to sleep?

I sigh and hang off the side of my mattress, staring at Lisa's empty bed. Has she even slept in it yet?

The professor kept the lid to the chest open tonight, so I can look out into the attic. I actually prefer it closed–the ceiling is decorated with glow-in-the-dark stars, so it's almost like being outside with them. Instead, I get to gaze up at the cobwebs hanging from the attic beams that have broken bicycles and sleds stored between them.

Maybe he's punishing me.

I roll over to the corner of my room and frown at the mirror. There's something on it, but I can't see well from this angle. I pull myself up and tiptoe towards it. It's been painted entirely in red, smeared with white strokes. I wipe the paint off with my finger, surprised by how fresh it is. I stand in front of it, startled when I realize that the white streaks aren't just random lines–it's a stick figure of a girl in a tutu…it's a stick figure of *me*.

"Couldn't smell the fumes, could you?" It's Lisa's voice, but childish and high-pitched. "Never look in the mirror–we are trapped in there."

I turn around and back into the mirror, the paint sticking to my dress. Lisa stands in the dark on her bed, a snapped paintbrush in hand. One end looks painfully sharp, the tip so pointed, it could easily pierce human skin.

"My spirit's sleeping somewhere cold." A new lisp to her voice, she tilts her head, contemplating something. "Freezing, freezing. But she's waking."

She vaults from the bed, landing with a thud, and brandishes the paintbrush above her head, wielding it like a knife as she ambles towards me.

"Lisa?" I raise my hands protectively. "Lisa, what's wrong?"

She doesn't respond, instead she continues towards me, forcing me into the corner of the chest.

"Lisa? I can help you! Just tell me what's wrong!"

"But *I'm* going to help *you*!" She titters, following abruptly with a throaty growl. She swipes at me and rips the strap of my leotard. It hangs by my shoulder, fuzzy threads appearing near the tear. "You have to let me break you—it shouldn't hurt for long."

I scream and crouch, covering my head when the paintbrush swings at me, then roll from the corner and leap onto my bed, looking down at her as she spins her weapon calmly in her hands.

"I don't want to be broken, Lisa." I try to ignore the tremble in my voice, but I sound shrill.

"You're already broken," Lisa enunciates, as if reasoning with a tot. "Destroying you completely is the only way you will be fixed."

Like a cat, she springs toward me, the paintbrush grasped in her hand like a joust. I dodge, the sharp end of the brush shredding the tip of my tutu.

I leap for the ladder and climb out of the chest, landing awkwardly on my toes with a telltale crack.

"What was that noise?" Lisa's muffled voice trails from inside the chest. "Are you breaking, dancing doll? You're not as new as you think."

I refrain from squealing in terror and launch towards the green chair, its usual sickly color camouflaged by the inky night. I scuttle beneath it, annoyed by the way my hips grind into one another with thunderous creaks. Thunderous to me, anyway—and all too audible to Lisa.

"I always know where you are." Her head pops up over the top of the chest, scanning the room. "Squeak, squeak, creak, creak, goes the dancing doll."

She throws herself from the chest and lands gracefully, taking cautious steps towards me even though I'm lost in the shadows.

What do I do? Hiding and running seem like the best options. If I can't do either, I have to fight back. I've never known how to fight—I don't even like watching it on TV.

Lisa creeps closer, silent lightning flashing on her vacant face. I turn to run, only to be violently hurled back against the leg chair.

My tutu is caught on a splinter and no amount of tugging frees it.

"Slowly and silently, cries the dancing doll, meekly, angelically, she weeps for her soul."

I pull down my tutu, leaving it stuck to the chair and canter as fast as I can, struggling with my perpetually pointed feet. Wait, I can leap! That's my only shot at outrunning Lisa.

I reach the attic door and glance at it, defeated by its size. I'll never reach it.

"Ella!" She says my name in her usual voice, husky and constantly irritated, and jogs towards me, the paintbrush leaning against her shoulder. "You're being silly, now. There's nowhere left to run!"

"There's always something…" I say through gritted teeth. I run my hand along the wall and sprint towards the dark corners in the attic. Lisa spent a lot of time there. Clearly, it's the perfect place to hide.

She runs behind me, but she isn't as fast. The professor didn't make her legs as long as mine.

The corner is littered with lots of tiny pieces of paper with writing on them. I'm not a great reader, but I recognize a few words like "experiment" and "trap".

"Don't read my notes!" Lisa cries, her feet slapping against the ground.

I ignore her and search frantically, desperate to find something– *anything*–that'd help me fight back.

There's a nail in the corner. It's rusted and heavy, but it's a weapon nonetheless. I bend over to pick it up and accidentally kick it instead. It rolls deeper into the darkness, seemingly forever. I chase it, but it's gone.

That doesn't make sense. Something can't just disappear like that! I get on all fours to crawl when I'm encompassed by complete darkness. I glance over my shoulder as Lisa searches for me with a confused look on her face.

"Did you find my mouse hole, dancer doll?" A demented smile doesn't reach her eyes. "It's a maze in there."

Mouse hole? Of course! The professor didn't plaster over them all! I check my surroundings and spot the dark tunnel, which is possibly the way out of the attic.

I quickly leap up and barge through the tunnel. I can't see a thing, but I don't slow down. I don't have *time* to slow down!

The tunnel narrows, so small now that I find myself bending over while I run. If I've never felt claustrophobic before, I definitely do now. I'm lost in the walls of my home with a psychopathic dolly on my tail. This isn't a story that can end well.

I smack into the wall, the dead-end—the nail in my coffin. I slap my hands on the surrounding walls, but they lead to nowhere.

"Took a wrong turn?" Lisa's voice echoes through the walls. "That's good. You won't see me when I break you. It'll be less upsetting."

A whimper escapes my throat. There's no point trying to hold it in–she already knows I'm here. Terrified, I slide down the wall and curl myself into a ball, preparing for my grizzly end.

There's a surprising amount of room down here, though. I don't have to stay in a ball at all – in fact, I can stretch out without touching the other wall.

I get on all fours and try to slap my hand against the barrier that's no longer there. Of course! Mice are short, they would only need small spaces to travel through! I crawl to the narrow opening and squeeze through, losing my left hand in the process. I can't say I care. It was a pathetically small hand, anyway.

I stand still in the open, gaping at the bright paneling in the hallway. It's much cozier than the attic. And then, there're three doors and the stairs. One has to lead to the professor's room, right?

"Ella! Come back!" Lisa screams through the walls. "Don't go to our maker!" She tries to slip through the crack, but gets wedged in halfway. She hits her free hand on the paneling to get my attention. "Ella! Seriously, stop! I'm trying to help you!"

Part of me feels compelled to yank her out–she looks so stranded, stuck in the wall like that. But the other half–

"—Ella! *RUN!*" Lisa points at something behind me. I turn and scream at the black cat that towers over me, its hiss volatile.

I don't know why I do what I do next. Somehow, coming head to head with an unpredictable beast has a higher success rate than spending another second with Lisa. I slide between the cat's paws and grip onto its tail, which thrashes me around. It growls and shoots down the stairs, desperate to get me off.

We reach the bottom and I release my grip, the cat slinking into the darkness. I stand and check the rest of my limbs. Apart from my missing hand, I seem to be okay. On the plus side, I *sort of* pet a cat–Gabby will be pleased that I ticked off another item on the bucket list.

I'm in what looks like a combined lounge room and kitchen. The professor has rather distinguished taste–the kitchen has marble tiles and countertops with wooden pantry doors. The lounge room is covered in various artworks and plants, with a glass coffee table and matching, grey couches. It's actually a lot more modern than I was expecting.

"Jupiter? Jupiter, what's all the fuss?"

A human's voice. I hide behind the banister when the lights switch on. Someone comes through the door by the lounge room, their eyes puffy and their hair ruffled. They're in a pink onesie which I don't care for. Onesies are inexplicitly in style again despite the revolting way they pull at the crotch.

"Jupiter? Come on, boy. Why were you growling like that?" The girl bends over to pick up the cat, stroking it gently.

Wait. That's Gabby! I emerge from my hiding place and jump on the spot. "Gabby! Down here! It's Ella!"

Gabby's eyes widen, and she drops the cat onto the couch. She rushes towards me and cups her palms so I can clamber up.

"Your hand! What happened?"

"The professor made another doll and she's *crazy*! She was trying to break me!" I cuddle into her hands. "Please, don't take me back up there. Why are you here? Do you live here?"

Gabby rolls her eyes. "My parents are away for the weekend, so I'm staying here. Are you telling me there's another human that's a doll?" When I nod, she continues. "And when you say she's trying to break you… does that mean she's trying to *kill* you?"

"I don't know!" I sit in her hand, biting my finger. "I don't know how any of this works! I don't understand how I was human and why I don't remember any of it! Everything was fine before Lisa showed up!"

"And Lisa is the crazy doll?"

"Yeah, she's a goth."

"Well, that probably explains a lot of her behavior."

I frown. Is this a joke? Being a goth shouldn't make anyone a killer. I bet it's the whole being turned into a doll and still remembering a past life that's made Lisa this way.

Gabby carries me into her bedroom, which looks remarkably plain, like the guestrooms on TV. Apricot walls, white bedspread, and a side table. Apart from that, there's nothing to really note.

She lowers me onto the bed and sits cross-legged on top of the covers. "So, why is she trying to kill you?" Her tone drips with both wonder and disgust.

I shrug and mimic her position. "She said it would help me. I don't know how dying could help anyone. I don't even know if I *can* die. I haven't aged in years. At least, I don't think I have. My head even fell off and the professor just had to screw it back on."

"Maybe she's jealous of how pretty you are and just wants to mangle you?"

"I've considered that. But… I think her actions run deeper than that. Oh, I'd hate to get the professor to deactivate her!"

"What does that mean?" Gabby leans over to the side table and takes a sip from the cup of water that's there. I watch in envy. If only I could remember what it was like to drink! The professor tries not to eat or drink in front of me to prevent me from desiring human needs. Could I ask Gabby to do the same thing? Or would it be totally rude?

"It means… I don't know what it means! He has to find her first—and that's the most difficult part. She has a remarkable skill of showing up when you don't want her and squirreling away when you need her. Once he has her, he'll take her into the lab and do… something that would stop her from walking and talking."

"So killing her, yeah?" Said with such ease, it metaphorically makes my stomach lurch.

"Yeah," I whisper. I don't want Lisa to die, but I can't have her chasing me around for the rest of my life. "I don't think the professor has ever done that before. Lisa's the only other human doll I've met."

Gabby shrugs. "Aunt Sianne used to say the professor crafted dolls all day and night. She hated it." I tilt my head to the side, mutely requesting a more in depth explanation. Gabby laughs. "*SO CUTE*. Anyway, Aunt Sianne died a while ago. Grandpa and she never got along too well. I never understood why she had such a grudge about him making dolls, but I never knew about you being human until yesterday."

I hesitate. "So, there are a lot of dolls that the professor has made?"

"According to Aunt Sianne, yeah. But she was a little loopy, kind of the black sheep of the family."

I don't know why her words trigger the onset of depression in me. It must've been the mention of family. I have no idea who my family is, or even if I have one. That's when it hits me: not only am I lonely… I'm actually *alone*.

"What's wrong?" Gabby strokes my arm, the one with the missing hand.

I shake my head and suck my lips, trying to impede the breathy moans that accompany crying. I don't last for long. Before I know it, I'm sobbing into my lap, unable to form jointed sentences.

"I... don't... know!" I push my hair from my face. I hate that it's not pinned in a bun tonight—it's just in the way now.

Gabby leans closer to me, pokes my cheek, and gasps.

"What?" I sniff.

"There's water on your face. I mean, tears are coming from your eyes. Are you supposed to do that?"

I instinctively stop weeping and wipe the moisture from my eyes. The small beads glisten on my fingertips. "Oh wow," I say, uncertain about the impossibility of tears. "I'm definitely not supposed to do that."

I laugh heartily, so much that I roll onto my back and clutch my stomach. "Nothing makes sense!" I giggle. Gabby is confused, but she laughs with me; the way sane people do to keep the crazies calm.

"Why are we laughing?" Gabby tries to smile, but it's more of a grimace.

"I don't know! Nothing makes sense!" I repeat hysterically. "I think I've gone mad!"

"We have a consensus!" Gabby chews her lip uncomfortably. "Ella, you're kind of scaring me."

"Sorry." I wipe away the remaining tears. "I'm just so confused about... life, I guess."

"Me too. Have you heard about the epidemic?"

I stand and nestle into Gabby's lap, the hysteria passing. "Bits and pieces. A lot of people are dying from it, but I don't really understand what it is."

"It's a virus that only affects those with a certain blood type," she says as if reading from a book. "O Positive is the most common blood type, and it's the only one that isn't immune to this virus." She pauses. "*I'm* O Positive."

"Yikes! Lucky you're not sick then!"

Gabby smiles tenderly and closes her eyes, squeezing out a single tear. "I am," she whispers.

I flinch. "What do you mean?"

"I'm part of the epidemic." More tears flow down her face. "That's why my parents made me stay here. Grandpa is the only one in our family that isn't O Positive, and my parents didn't want me to suffer in quarantine. They'd rather I be in a comfortable place when…" She trails off. "I'm not contagious anymore, you know. *Everyone* knows you can only infect people in the first week, but my parents are cowards. They don't want to be near me when…"

I study her face, only now noticing the toll the illness had taken on her body. I thought her pale complexion was beautiful and healthy, but now I acknowledge the lack of color in her lips and her gaunt cheekbones. This whole time I envied her for being human, when now I pity her for it.

"What does it do to you?" I ask slowly, stroking her hand with mine.

"Kills me." She shrugs, unable to look at anything but her feet. "Makes me lose weight. I have these awful headaches, then my stomach hurts. After a while, your body just shuts down. The doctors say I have no chance. My immune system isn't strong enough."

"That's why you wanted to make that bucket list! It wasn't for me, was it?"

She doesn't respond, craning her neck to look through the blinds and at the storm that's still going strong. "There's a ballet tomorrow that I've had tickets to for months, but Grandpa thinks I'm too weak to go."

"You look fine to me?"

"I know." She grins. "I'm a good actor. Truth be told, every muscle in my body is screaming in agony right now."

"But how do you catch it?"

"They only have theories so far," Gabby says. "Some believe it's airborne, others think it could be vaccinations gone wrong. I started showing symptoms after I swam in the public pool three weeks ago."

I wince before uttering the next question. "How long do you have?"

"They usually say you have a month before the body shuts down. We're guessing I have one week left." She smiles weakly and scratches at her nose. "So I'm not going to waste a single second crying about it. I'm going to live life to the fullest! And you know what? I'm going to start by going to the ballet! Life is about quality, right?"

"Great idea!" I say encouragingly, but I know the professor won't allow it. My tone mustn't have been convincing, though, because Gabby's eyebrows furrow.

"You don't think he'll let me, do you?" She slumps in defeat.

"You know how overprotective he is. I mean, he's never even let me leave the attic," I whisper. "But I can perform for you! I know all the moves! We'll make our own ballet!"

Gabby beams. "Okay! Just promise me you'll go to the ballet anyway? It might be your only chance to ever see a live one."

I scoff. "What are you talking about?"

"Grandpa is going to the ballet." Gabby's voice rises in excitement. "You can sneak into his coat and tell me what it was like! Please? You *have* to! *Then* you can come home and perform the whole thing over for me! I'll make a stage for you out of my shoebox!"

"I don't know…" I mumble, not fond of breaking the rules again.

"Ella, please? We only have a week left together…" Gabby's nostrils flare and her lips quiver.

I rub the back of my neck. "I tell you what; if the professor lets you go, then I'll come with you. But *only* if he lets you go. Deal?"

Gabby raises her pinkie finger and wraps it around my arm. "Promise." She yawns and gently lowers herself into bed, kneading her cushion like a cat. "Will you sleep next to me? Wake me up if that crazy doll comes near you again, okay?"

I smile, even though she probably can't see my expressions in the darkness. My gaze lingers on her innocent, sickly face. I can't work out if I'm lucky to have her by my side, or cursed knowing she'll soon be gone.

"Okay," I promise quietly.

Her eyelids flutter, droop and suddenly, she is gone from this world.

CHAPTER SIX

GABBY. NEVER GAB.

The deer watches me. He's evil. He has to be. I swear he's smiling at me... mockingly. He's the only thing I can make out in the darkness. I know there are trees around, but only because of the way they rustle in the wind.

I sit in the middle of the road, too distraught to stand. There's a white light up ahead, just behind the deer. Maybe if I crawl towards it, everything will be okay...

I decided to hide beneath the bed before Gabby woke up. All girls need privacy first thing in the morning to brush their hair, dress, and take down the puffy swelling below their eyes. I figured it was the polite thing to do before I ask her to take me back to the attic–being there was no way in the world I could go up there alone. I considered telling the professor, but he would probably freak out if he knew I spent the whole night downstairs. Why? I don't know. His controlling nature is only becoming more apparent the more I spend time with Gabby and Lisa.

It stopped raining halfway through the night. The sky was still grey and droplets of rain remained on the window, but the storm had moved on.

"Ella?" Gabby calls. I remain seated, flicking the ribbons on my shoes. "Ella?"

She sounds panicked so I stand and push back the sheet that hangs by the bed. "Yeah?"

Gabby kneels on her bed, her eyes beady and red. "I thought you'd left me!"

"Never." I climb up the sheet to join her on the bed. "But the girls on TV like their privacy as they are getting dressed."

"I hadn't even woken up yet!" She protests, nudging me on the shoulder. "Here, let me show you something!"

Gabby groans as she supports her weight on the bedpost to stand, then shuffles towards the built-in cupboard and tugs on the doorknob. When it opens, she drops to her knees and rummages through a box on the ground.

I walk towards her and stand on tiptoes to look inside.

Gabby pulls out a dress that is the size of a human foot made from floaty material with large cerulean and iridescent stripes, it takes my eye immediately. A midnight blue sash is tied around the waist, complementing the sweetheart neckline.

"It matches your eyes." Gabby lowers the dress into my hands. "The aqua parts, anyway. Not so much the green. Oooh, you'll look lovely if you tie your hair back into an elegant knot. The way your hair is now doesn't suit you."

I stare at the dress, completely enamoured by its beauty. "What's this for?"

"For the ballet tonight, dummy!" Gabby motions for me to turn around. When I comply, she runs her fingers through my hair and pins it back. "Every young lady should have a nice dress to wear, and I've only ever seen you in tutus. This belonged to my doll Sally, but I think you need it more than she does."

A lump metaphorically forms in my throat. I want to cry again, even though I'm not sad. I never understood why women on TV burst into tears when they were happy, but it's starting to make sense. Just one thoughtful, generous act and suddenly, it feels like the whole world is at my feet.

"Thank you," I whisper, unable to suppress the tremble in my voice. "It's perfect."

We collectively flinch when the door upstairs slams and the professor's footsteps clobber down the steps.

"Uh-oh. You have to hide me, Gab!"

"Firstly, it's Gabby, never Gab," she says. "Secondly, what are you talking about? Can't we tell him the truth?"

"No." I run towards the bed. "He'll hate that I spent the night here and didn't tell him."

Gabby rolls her eyes and lifts me from the ground. She cradles me in her hands and shakes her head. "Ella, a flipping psychopath doll tried to break you. Tell him she pushed you down the stairs and you couldn't get back up. It'll be okay."

The door smacks into the wall when the professor pants in the doorway, unaccustomedly flustered. He spots me, and smiles for a fraction of a second, before his face droops.

"Why are you here?" His voice is scratchy, like he needs a drink.

Nervously, I cuddle into Gabby's hands. "Please, don't get mad. I didn't have a choice."

"Yeah," Gabby chimes in, her voice melodic betwixt the distress. The professor's eyes dart to and fro like he's watching a tennis match. "Grandpa, what we're about to tell you is a little discon... disconcerting, I think the word is. You know Lisa, that goth doll, right? Yeah, well, she pretty much vowed to destroy Ella last night. She was coming at her all psycho like, so Ella ran to get to you, but Lisa pushed her down the stairs! I came out because I heard Jupiter meowing, so I rescued her. I was going to get you, but... well, you've been tired lately, and I didn't want to wake you. So I figured we'd tell you in the morning."

The professor sweeps back what's left of his hair that's stuck to his forehead. He walks up to us, arms outstretched, and plucks me out of Gabby's hands. "But you're both okay?" He asks a full minute later. When we nod, he reciprocates. "Good. Do you know where Lisa is now? I haven't seen her since I activated her."

"No," Gabby and I say in unison.

"Well we need to find her!" The professor's voice rises. "She's found a way to get out of the attic, which means she could be anywhere! Close all doors and windows and do *not* let her escape! If you find her, let me know."

Gabby scratches her nose. "Ella said you'll deactivate her for the whole attempted murder thing."

The professor looks down at me fondly, lightly tapping my head with his finger. "All things have a purpose, whether it be to create chaos or bring hope. I wished that Lisa would be my bundle of hope, but she's nothing more than hopelessly chaotic." He pauses. "She must be stopped."

Despite the fleeting relief, I can't help but dread the moment when Lisa is deactivated. She's not evil–just troubled.

Does anyone who causes trouble really deserve to die?

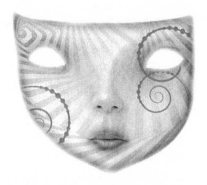

CHAPTER SEVEN

BUT IT WAS HOME

S o what do we do exactly?" Gabby presses the record button. She kneels next to me, leaning in to speak into the microphone. "This thing is like a billion years old! I should give you my tablet."

"A tablet? No thanks, pills wouldn't work on me anyway," I decline kindly. "It's imagination time." I clap my hands together. "It's where anything can and anything *does* happen! Sometimes I pretend I'm a spy infiltrating the attic to find the mysterious stone or... or I'm in the jungle riding a saber-toothed tiger!"

"So what are we imagining today?"

"That we're traveling gypsies with magical powers," I whisper, widening my eyes. "I'm Trixie, and you're Kali! We're sisters on the run from the demonic witch, Victor!"

Gabby grins. "That sounds like a book!"

"It's a work in progress." I giggle. "Okay, let's start!"

"Wait! What are my powers?"

"Pretty much anything. You're stronger than me because you're connected to Victor." I breathe in and begin to imagine Gabby and myself in carnival clothes with colorful corsets and laced boots.

"What's the go with Victor? Like, why is he after us?"

"Because he hates that he doesn't have power over us," I say quickly, annoyed that we're not jumping straight into the fun. "He's trying to control us with magic. He hates Kali the most because she's strong-willed and fights against him. She lives a life of her own and is happier for it. Trixie is the softer sister, who isn't as powerful. Victor completely brainwashes her into doing his bidding."

Gabby frowns and awkwardly scratches at her elbow. "That's intense. Is it just me, or does he sound like Grandpa?"

My beautiful carnival disappears. The corsets fade. Gabby's platinum pigtails return to her unkempt style. All I see is the attic, grey and dusty. I remain silent, Gabby's words ringing in my head.

"Ella? Ella, I'm sorry! I didn't mean anything by it! It was just an observation!" Gabby tilts her head to the side, her eyebrows furrowing.

I shake my head and press the pause button on the recorder. "It's okay. We should probably get ready for the ballet, anyway."

"No! I want to play imagination time. Look, I'm a gypsy! Woosh, go my magical powers!"

"You should brush your hair," I say quietly, staring at the dead flowers in the corner of the room that the professor never removed.

Gabby chews the side of her lip, a concerned or guilty look on her face—I can't figure out which. She stands and leaves, her walk slow.

I sit alone, wondering about my story. I never had a title for it, but one just popped into my head.

Brainwashed.

The dress is more beautiful than anything I could ever imagine. I almost look human in it. Its full length covers my hinged knees and stick-thin legs. Unfortunately, it only seems to highlight my missing hand, but that's fixable. The professor will get a new one for me tomorrow.

I twirl in the mirror that the professor wiped down for me. The dress lifts and floats down, like a feather.

It is a good distraction from the foggy, plastic box the professor has put over the chest. He said Lisa won't be able to infiltrate it and I should be safe while they're at the ballet. I hate the stupid box! My voice sounds muffled in here, and I can barely see through it.

The door clicks closed, and I freeze, then rush towards the bed and wrap the blanket around me, fearful that the professor will not be satisfied until I explain why I'm in such a lovely dress.

"Ella?" An outline of Gabby shows through the plastic. She lifts it up and frowns. "Why's it so dark in here? I can't have this!" She leans over and turns on the flashlight in the chest, illuminating the small area. She looks immaculate. The professor has let her wear red lipstick to match the red, flowing skirt. The top half of her dress is covered in silver sequins, the straps hidden by her curled hair.

"He's letting you go to the ballet? How did you convince him?" I jump onto my bed. "You look very pretty, by the way."

"Thank you." She twinkles. "It was actually pretty easy to guilt him into it. All I had to say was I've only got one week left to enjoy the small things in life, and he folded."

I cringe. It bugs me, how blasé she is about her terminal illness. Most of it is probably an act, but it's almost like she doesn't appreciate being human.

Gabby reaches for her handbag and opens it. Excluding the gold strap, it fits her outfit to a T. "Okay, get in!"

I climb up the ladder and look down at the purse. There's not going to be a lot of room for me in there. It looks so dark and tight, it reminds me of my traumatic experience in the mouse hole.

"Gabrielle? Where are you?" The professor is outside.

"Crap! Hurry, hurry!" Gabby waves for me to get in the bag.

I close my eyes and dive into the darkness. The opening clicks shut behind me the moment I land. I barely have time to get used to my surroundings before Gabby begins to walk. "Coming, Grandpa!"

The door screeches, and we've left the attic.

I'm not excited about the ballet. To be honest, the dancers have barely crossed my mind. I've been far too preoccupied with the possibility of getting into trouble. I shift so that I'm on the flat of my back. Luckily, Gabby didn't put anything else in the purse–only a handful of coins.

"Where were you?" the professor asks when Gabby reaches the bottom of the stairs.

"Saying goodbye to Ella. I said I'd take notes for her so she can practice new dance moves."

I shake my head. How can she lie easily to her grandfather?

Keys jangle, and Gabby and the professor step outside.

"I love my little broken doll," the professor says. I can't see him, but a smile warms his voice. "She would've loved the ballet."

"Why not let her come, then?" Gabby throws the purse into the car before following suit. I bounce around and readjust my position.

The professor closes his door and starts up the engine. "Can you imagine what society would think if they found a walking, talking doll? She'd be taken away from us."

"Couldn't she pretend to be a real doll? You know, inanimate?"

It's odd, hearing people talk about you when you're not supposed to be there. It's both flattering and nerve-wracking that at any given minute, you'll hear something you won't like.

"And what kind of life would that be? Pretending to be something you're not?" the professor asks. The car rocks as we swerve out onto the road.

"Probably better than a life where nothing happens," Gabby mumbles. "Seriously, Grandpa. It's kind of ridiculous not letting her ever leave the attic."

"Gabby, you don't understand!" His voice is tight. "It's what she wanted!"

No way! I assume Gabby is as stunned as I am because she doesn't reply. Just as well. I wouldn't know what to ask him. He has to be lying. Who'd want a lonely eternity in the attic?

The silence is broken when the radio comes on. The music is calm and sweet, with a slow beat and soothing bass. It must be what gives Gabby the confidence to speak.

"Why do you call Ella a broken doll?" She picks up the purse and sits it on her lap. How does she know I find being in people's laps comforting?

"Because that's what she is." The professor is harder to hear over the music. I really wish he'd learn to speak through his diaphragm.

"But how?" Gabby presses. "She's missing a hand, sure, but she's not broken."

"You didn't know her when she was human."

Gabby doesn't respond. Instead, as the music picks up, she clips open the purse and glances at me with a confused expression. I shrug and mouth 'I don't know'. I never met myself as a human— whom am I to tell if I wasn't a completely different person?

The streetlamps blind me as we pass them. Gabby notices me squinting and closes her purse, once again leaving me in what feels like an eternal void.

The car slows, and Gabby leans to the left when we turn into, assumingly, a parking lot. The engine's purr abruptly cuts off, and Gabby and the professor hurry out.

People murmur nearby as the car lock engages, and the bumps that accompany Gabby's bouncy way of walking tell me we are going inside.

"Sure is busy tonight," Gabby says, and the professor responds with a disinterested grunt.

Very slowly, a stream of light pours into the handbag as Gabby unlatches the lock. I crouch and peek over the rim, noting their tenseness.

It's not fair that they're fighting over me. Maybe, I shouldn't have come. At least, this way I wouldn't feel guilty about their quarrel.

I don't dwell on their squabble for long. I'm far too gobsmacked by the size of the theatre up ahead to focus on anything else.

It's big–well, obviously–and really modern. The theatres I've seen on TV are rustic and adorned with gargoyles or something. *This* theatre looks like an abstract piece of rock that's conveniently landed in the right place at the right time.

We enter the foyer, golden lights and crimson carpet only enhancing the posh, glamorous vibe. The professor is immediately greeted by a waiter who offers a glass of sparkling wine. The professor kindly refuses and places a tender hand on Gabby's shoulder.

"I'm sorry for the harsh words exchanged, dear," he says softly. "I love you."

"Love you too," Gabby replies matter-of-factly and strokes his hand.

"You're very brave." The tears well up in the professor's eyes.

Gabby shrugs. "Don't have a choice. I think Libby's braver."

"Who is Libby?"

Gabby points to a girl her age, surrounded by family. The girl has no hair and is wearing a bandana tightly around her head. Her skin is as dark as Lisa's clothing, and her eyebrows are non-existent. She is frail, but she doesn't stop smiling. I don't think anyone should stop smiling.

"She's sick, like me, but with something as old as time. She's been in and out of the hospital her whole life and said the next time she goes in will be her last. I haven't worked out if she's just trying to be positive in a bad situation." Gabby licks her lips. "I'm thirsty. May I please get a lemonade?"

Libby must hear Gabby's voice, because her eyes glisten when she waves her hand dramatically over her head, calling out. She walks towards Gabby to embrace her, her teeth glorious pearls.

"Lovely to see you here!" Libby's voice is deep and angelic.

"You too. When did you come out of hospital?" Gabby nods at the hospital gown that hangs past Libby's red coat.

"Thirty minutes ago." Libby laughs. "I'm going back in tonight. I didn't want to spend my birthday in bed."

I glance at the professor who is eyeing Libby a little too intensely. His narrowed eyes, pursed lips, and flared nostrils would give me goosebumps if I had skin.

"How old are you?" He crosses his arms.

Libby doesn't seem perturbed by the curtness. "I'm twelve today, sir."

"And you're terminal, correct?" If I had been drinking water, I would've spit it out. Did he really just ask a kid if she's terminal? Who *does* that?

"I don't see it that way, sir." Libby smiles, but the sadness tinges her voice. "My adventure may end here, but it shall continue elsewhere."

"Hmm," he mumbles.

Really? That's all the professor can say? 'Hmm'? What's *wrong* with him tonight?

The lights flicker, followed by a cheery ding.

"Oh, the show's about to begin!" Libby's face lights up. She hugs Gabby and inexplicably curtsies to the professor. There's no way in the world I would have been polite to him after the way he conducted himself. "Have a lovely time!"

When she's out of earshot, the professor bends down to Gabby. "What is her full name?"

"Libby Cox." Gabby frowns, visibly unsettled by the professor's behavior.

"And how do you know her?"

"From school, before she got sick."

The professor hesitates. "Do you like her?"

"Yeah, she's nice." Gabby shifts and pokes her finger through the purse. She wiggles it, so I know she's seeking reassurance. I wrap my arms around it and cuddle her finger, hoping it's enough. "So, about that lemonade?"

"You head inside, Gabrielle. I'll get you that drink." The professor pats her softly on the shoulder before walking against the flow of theatergoers to reach the bar.

Gabby enters through a set of grand doors and opens the purse wider for me to view the inside. The stage is magnificent—everything I could've ever wished to perform on. The starlit ceiling shines down on the fake vines wrapped around the columns, and the seats look expensive. Like really, expensive. I'd be too nervous to drink in case I spilled anything on the fabric.

Gabby squeezes through the fourth aisle and settles in her seat. "Seriously! What is wrong with Grandpa?" she whispers, trying not to look at me when she speaks. I presume it's because she doesn't want people to think she is talking to her crotch. "That was so...so..."

"I know!" I whisper too, semi-paranoid about being seen. I keep my nose rested on the tip of the purse, using that as my visibility cut-off. "If this were a movie, I'd suspect him of being the creepy stalker or killer. I just... I don't know; things are sucking lately."

"Preaching to the choir, Ella." Gabby leans against the armrest. "But, we're finally here. It's another one for the bucket list. Everything is beautiful at the ballet..."

Gabby was wrong. Nothing was beautiful at the ballet. It was better than that.

Graceful men lifted lovely girls in white, and princes swooned over their swans. Whenever a ballerina raised her arms, someone was always there to catch her.

The live music was so much better than the deteriorating TV

speakers. The orchestra was like a romantic radioactive wave that wafted through the theater, sending ripples of emotion through the audience.

The dancers' technique was flawless, impeccable, *perfect*. I loved how their eyes glistened when the audience cheered. I envied their heaving chests as they posed during the applause. I wanted the exquisitely crafted costumes that pressed into their flesh. *They have a life.*

I put my hand to my mouth and sob. This time, not because I'm happy. I'm crying because of fury, envy... *hatred*. I don't want to tear my gaze away from the beauty, but I can't bear to watch a life that isn't mine.

Tears run down my cheeks as I curl into a small ball in the purse. Gabby prods my side, but I cover my face with my good hand. I'm beyond words.

"Grandpa, I have to use the bathroom," Gabby whispers.

"Oh!" The professor sounds shocked. "Should I come with you?"

"No, no, it's fine. You enjoy!"

The track feels like an eternity. I don't notice or care where we're going. It's only when Gabby clamps her hand around my waist and sits me on top of the sink in a room filled with cubicles and glaring white tiles that I calm down.

"What's going on?" Her voice is exasperated. She leans on one leg, her arms rested crossly on her hips. "I thought you would like this!"

I sniff, too ashamed to look her in the eye. I fiddle with my stump (man, I wish I knew where my hand was) and kick my dress as I swing my legs.

"I don't want to be this way anymore, Gabby," I mumble. "I always imagined being human again, but I never realized how much I despised being a doll. I always thought it was cool that I never felt pain or aged, but since meeting you... Gabby, I'm not living. I'm dead. What if I *am* dead? Maybe, Lisa is doing me a favor by trying to kill me! I can't go on like this!"

"Whoa, ease up!" Gabby swipes at my cheeks with her thumb. "When I said I wasn't going to waste any more time on tears, I didn't just mean my own. Ella, you're immortal. Do you know how much I wish I could be like you? I have a week to live, and here you're complaining that your life isn't perfect!"

I bite my bottom lip and nod slowly. "Gabby, I'm so sorry."

"Don't be sorry." She lifts me from the sink and lowers me into her purse. "Just be grateful."

I stare at her from the purse, a warm feeling pulsating in my chest. She really cares about me; maybe about as much as I care about her. "I *am* grateful," I say softly. "Gabby? I know this sounds weird, considering we haven't known each other for long… and I'm really sorry for saying this… but, I, um… I…"

"I love you, too." Gabby lifts her purse to kiss my head.

I can't stop grinning. For some illogical reason, I now feel like I can take on the world.

Is it possible to watch something without ever really seeing it? Because that's what happened when I tried to watch the remainder of the ballet. I was too busy gathering old memories from my human life. Well, truth be told, I was only making them up. I liked the concept of horse-riding and gymnastics, but I'm not sure why.

I applauded half-heartedly when the dancers bowed and smiled nostalgically at the drawn curtain. My first and last visit to the ballet hadn't been the soiree I envisioned, but it probably beat sitting alone in a plastic box avoiding Lisa.

"Hey! It's Libby!" Gabby says when we reach our car. I peek through the opening in the purse and sure enough, Libby's beaming four cars down.

"I don't see you for months, and now you can't get rid of me!" Libby blows Gabby a kiss. "Good luck, bud. See ya on the other side."

Gabby doesn't reply, she only waves and throws herself in the backseat of the car.

The professor turns the on the ignition, muffling the outside voices. "What did you think, Gabrielle? Did you enjoy yourself?"

Gabby pauses, tightening her lips. "I loved it."

"I'm glad, sweetheart." He reverses out of the parking space. We drive for the length of two modern contemporary songs playing on the radio, before the professor takes a deep breath. "I liked your friend." His voice is higher than usual, and he sniffs after he speaks.

Gabby exchanges a worried look with me and tents her fingers in her lap. "I know."

CHAPTER EIGHT

RUSH

The floorboards beneath the carpet creak as Gabby climbs the stairs. She's clutching her handbag and keeping it close to her heart, her eyes darting from the attic door to me.

"I'm going upstairs to say goodnight to Ella," Gabby calls to the professor.

"Hey!" I hiss from the purse. "Why'd you say that?"

"What?" She breathes. "He's going to hear me go into the attic anyway and wonder what I'm doing!"

"But now he'll come running up here!"

On cue, hurried footsteps follow us upstairs. "No! She's probably asleep! Don't disturb her!"

"Run!"

I position myself in the purse to avoid the pending earthquake. Gabby bolts for the door, jiggling the handle until it unlatches. The door swings closed behind her, and she crashes into a box in the dark. She grunts and hops through the pain until she reaches the chest. She drops me onto my bed and kneels beside the chest, breathing heavily through her nose. "Get in the bed! He'll see your dress! Hide!"

Of course! I dive under the covers and nuzzle into the pillow, attempting to look dazed by my alleged interrupted sleep.

"Gabrielle!" The professor trips over the same fallen box. His hair is crazed, wild, and his words run into one another. "What are you doing? Why did you close the door?"

Gabby places a tender finger to her lips and points to me.

"Shh. You'll wake Ella. You're right, Grandpa, I should've let her sleep. Let's go to bed." Gabby clears her throat and stands on tiptoes to kiss the professor's cheek.

She leaves the attic, and the professor remains confused and motionless, swaying above the chest. I stare up at him from my bed, only now noticing his change of attire. I'm so accustomed to seeing him in drab clothes that I almost don't recognize him in his collared shirt and dress pants. He looks quite presentable—handsome, almost.

When he looks down at me, I close my eyes and pretend to be asleep. He doesn't bother to kiss me goodnight like he usually does.

He knows…

CHAPTER NINE

MEET SIANNE

I fold the dress Gabby gave me into a neat square on the end of the bed and slip back into my leotard. My tutu is still caught on the chair where Lisa tried to track me down, and I don't really want to leave the safety of the chest to retrieve it.

It's actually kind of boring alone in the chest. I've never really spent that much time in it. I always have free reign of the attic to watch TV, paint, and look through the window. In here, there's literally nothing to do but pull faces in the mirror. Even then, my plastic skin can't do much. I've mastered raising one eyebrow at a time, but that's the extent of my facial versatility.

"It must be horrible only having one hand."

I feel like I've just been thrown into an icy lake. I remain stiff on the bed, unable to glance over my shoulder. "I found it for you." The voice is kind, soft... *fake.*

I place my hand on my chest when a tiny drum pounds from the inside. My heart is beating... "How?" I ask breathlessly, my pulse racing.

"Before the professor put the plastic box over the chest, I came in and hid under the bed." Lisa crawls over the covers to sit next to me. "I needed to talk to you. Did you have fun at the ballet?"

"No," I reply, only able to respond one word at a time. My eyes widen at Lisa who holds my detached hand in her lap. She lifts it and screws it into my stump, her expression not as ominous as it had been yesterday.

"No? That's not good." She inspects my hand to ensure it's in place. "Why not?"

I stare at her, unable to close my mouth. My pulse subsides to inexistence again, but my limbs still feel cold.

Lisa sighs and sweeps her fringe to the side, then sits back with her hands squeezed between her knees. "I'm so sorry." She shakes her head, blinking at the ground. "I don't know what came over me. You have to understand I wasn't myself. I'm not coping with this human-to-doll transition thing. My brain... it's like it's not working properly. Maybe, it never worked properly in my human form. I don't know."

Of course, she isn't coping. It's been an eternity, but I'm starting to resent being a doll myself.

"I found something when I explored the attic the other day," Lisa continues. I flinch when she puts her hand on my knee and instinctively inch away from her, but she doesn't seem to notice and only leans closer. "It sparked something. I think, that's why I went crazy. I need to show you."

"Just tell me." My voice cracks as I speak. There's something about the distressed way Lisa talks that doesn't make me question her.

The attic door creaks open, and the lights turn on. Lisa leaps from her position and crawls beneath the bed. I remain in place and smile when the professor appears. He lifts the plastic box and bends over to stroke my hair.

"Professor? It's the middle of the night. Can't you sleep?"

"No." His voice is gravelly, and his eyes have dark rings beneath them, as if he's been awake for days. "I didn't say goodnight to you, and it troubled me."

I smile, the coldness in my limbs slowly fading away. "Goodnight, professor."

He removes his glasses and cleans them with his cardigan. "Truth be told, there was an ulterior motive to my visit. I made you something." He digs in the pocket of his cord pants and pulls out a tiny, white plastic necklace with a red button. He throws it over my head and grins. "That's a panic button, just in case Lisa shows up and you need help."

I stroke the edges of the button by my throat. Should I press it right now? One tiny slip, and Lisa would be history.

Reluctantly, I drop my hands to my waist. I can't kill Lisa. Not yet. Not when she claims to know something revolutionary. The professor frowns.

"You found your hand?"

I panic, but only for a second. "Yeah. Can you believe it was in the chest the whole time? Silly me!" I'm getting way too used to lying.

"Oh," the professor says, the skepticism in his voice painfully obvious. "So, what did you get up to whilst we were away?"

I shrug. "Just the usual. I slept, I danced. Nothing to report."

"I'm sure." He looks down his nose at me. "Well, then. Goodnight, my broken doll."

"Thanks for the button, professor," I say as I watch him take long, unhurried steps to the light switch.

Once he turns out the lamp and closes the door, Lisa pops up. "Get rid of that stupid thing!"

I position my finger on the button threateningly. "Tell me what's going on."

She scrunches her hair with her hands, as if about to pull it out. "I told you, I have to show you!"

"Don't think I won't press it." I feel surprisingly powerful with my button. This is a much better weapon than that rusted nail I tried to use yesterday.

Lisa huffs and rubs her shoulders. "You're not going to believe me unless I show you."

"Tell me first, and then I'll decide whether I want to see it," I say diplomatically.

"There's *another* doll," Lisa blurts. She slumps over and flicks her shoelace. "Another *human* doll who remembers her past life. Here, in this attic."

My eyes flutter while I try to process the information. "Sorry?"

Lisa flops her head into her hands and groans. "See! I knew you wouldn't believe me!"

"I'm just... trying to understand." It's like I've temporarily forgotten how to speak English. "How come we never knew about her?"

"That's what I want to know." Lisa's eyes narrow as she drops her voice. "The professor isn't all hugs and kittens. He's evil. Who in their right mind would take an ordinary girl and make her a doll, confining them to an attic? It's preposterous!"

I fiddle with my recently attached hand. "Where is she?"

"She's in a box... in another box... a shoebox." Lisa rolls her eyes. "That *professor* had her in solitary confinement for years! I don't know what sick game he's playing, but he's dressed her just like him. She has a lab coat, glasses, everything!"

I clench my hands into fists and whip up. "You're lying. Take me to her right now!"

Lisa smirks and stands so that she's at my eyelevel. "I'd hoped you'd say that. Ladies first." She motions towards the ladder out of the chest.

I shoot her a disgusted look before I climb onto the ladder. The plastic box has a gap between the chest and the floor, so I slide down and squeeze until I'm wedged free.

Lisa follows closely behind with a triumphant smirk. "Careful with that button. Seriously, don't press it, otherwise we'll never get to the bottom of this. Now follow me!"

Lisa takes small steps, but walks quickly, like someone desperate to go to the bathroom. She heads towards the dark corner–the same one I escaped through the mouse hole. Oh, that was horrid! What am I even doing following her? This must be a trap! I'm so stupid...

A foreign language breaks up my pity-fest. It's in low murmurs and never stops for a break. I look at Lisa for reassurance, but she only raises her finger to her lips. She leads me through the gaps between the towering boxes until we reach a small space. A flashlight leans against one of the boxes, several paintbrushes, a pile of tissues, and a doll sitting with her knees pressed against her chest, rocking backward and forth. Her hair is long, messy, and grey with dust. Her lab coat looks like it used to be white, but it's covered in grime and dead bugs.

"Forty seven hundred thousand, three hundred and twenty two... no!" She hits her temples with her fists. "No, no, no! Forty seven hundred thousand, three hundred and ninety, ninety... no!"

"She remembers you," Lisa whispers.

My whole world shifts and collapses beneath my feet. My heart shatters at the thought of this poor woman being locked away for years.

Lisa was right. The professor is evil.

I creep closer, incapable of speaking.

"Hey," Lisa says slightly louder, clicking her fingers to grab the doll's attention. The doll's head shoots up, and she cackles like a witch.

"You're back! They said I'd be alone, be alone again, you know? You do know. Ha... you always know." She speaks quickly at first, until her tone swiftly shifts from fast-paced to suspicious. The doll turns her nose in the air. "I see you brought the chosen one?"

"Sianne, this is Ella. There's something you want to tell her, isn't there?" Lisa speaks cautiously.

Sianne sniffs, like some kind of wild animal. I highly doubt she can actually smell anything. "*Ella...*" She says, before muttering something incoherent, then puts her hands to the ground and slides her feet so that she is sitting at a right angle. "My dear Ella! My long-lost daughter!"

My chest suddenly feels tight. Sianne's my mother? I have a family? That can't be right...

"Well?" Sianne taps her fingers impatiently. "Come, child! Don't delay our reunion!"

I don't move. "You're not my mother."

"And how would you know?" Lisa snaps. "You don't remember your human life!"

"I know." I watch Sianne. The professor painted our faces similarly. We have the same color eyes and nose–the only disparity is the mole above her lip. Her wig reaches her waist, thick layers clumping together–it's a botched job. She looks just like me. "But she's not my mother."

When I don't budge, Sianne stands and shuffles over to me, tilting her head to the side. "We watched the full moon rise, and then began the lies. Imagine our surprise, when I ordered curly fries. No..." She growls and taps her head. "We went over this, Sianne! That's not how the story goes!"

I shift uncomfortably and look at Lisa for support. She nods at me, motioning for me to interact.

"Sianne," I try to sound soothing, but my voice trembles. "Did you used to work with the professor? Is that why you wear that lab coat?"

Her right eye widens, and her left eye twitches. "Don't utter his name! Daniel! Daniel was his name. Yes, yes the professor. We used to experiment all the time. He showed me how to do things and I said... I said stop. I said *please* stop. And you know what?"

She pauses, waiting for me to respond.

"What?"

She leans closer, cupping her hands around her mouth. "He *didn't* stop," she breathes. "Obsessed. Obsessed with dollies he was. Still is."

"But why did he put you away?"

"Isn't it obvious?" She throws her arms in the air, baring her teeth. "I broke the rules, didn't I? I remembered *everything*. I rebelled. Look at her!" Sianne points at Lisa. "*She's* rebelling! Now he'll want to deactivate her! That's just what he does! He knows everything you do and he *judges* everything. Don't think he doesn't know you weren't at the ballet!"

My stomach lurches—but not metaphorically this time. I actually feel it churning and squirming. I instinctively cuddle my waist, desperate for the nausea to dissipate. "What do you mean?"

"He knows you went to the ballet," Lisa says, emerging from the shadows. "And if you keep breaking the rules, he'll deactivate you."

"Or worse," Sianne says. "He'll put you away. Away in a box, just like me, forever. Staring into the darkness, wondering when and if you'll ever see sunlight again. I didn't speak until Lisa found me. The voices in my head were loud enough—I didn't want to add another..."

"But how does he know I went to the ballet? I was concealed!" I shriek. Is this what hysteria feels like?

"He knows *everything*!" Lisa folds her arms. I can't work out if she's annoyed at *me*, or the situation.

"He'll probably deactivate you when he sees you next," Sianne says nonchalantly, blowing on the tips of her hair and sitting back down. "There's a lot more, you know."

I hesitate, not sure whether I want to know more. "A lot more what?"

"Dollies," Sianne says, in a manner that is akin to an arrogant teenager sarcastically drawling '*Really?* You didn't *know that?*'

Oh boy, I really wish I'd never asked. I feel dizzy, flushed and... unwell. I fan my face and exhale.

"You're starting to feel more human, aren't you?" Lisa watches me like a lioness on the hunt. "The more dolls that are activated, the more we start to feel human. My throat and wrists have been aching really badly for the past few hours. The pain has increased over the last couple of days. I'm starting to wonder if the professor has activated another doll."

I stop listening. I don't want to hear any more of their conspiracy theories. All I want is to get back to Gabby and spend the little time I have left with her.

"Has Ella seen the closet?" Sianne looks at Lisa, who only shakes her head.

"She's seen nothing." Lisa's tone drips with disgust. "I'm going to take her there now. Will you come with us?"

Sianne sighs and rubs her eyes. "The guardians told me I wouldn't like it, not without popcorn, no way. But I'll come. I've spent too much time away from my daughter." She attempts to squeeze my hand, but I pull away. "Help me up!"

I reluctantly reach for Sianne and pull her up, startled by how short she is. She only comes up to my shoulder.

"Come on," Lisa snaps, taking a left turn past the tower of boxes. Sianne holds my tutu and follows behind as we weave in the dark. We reach what I think is a dead-end until Lisa points towards the ceiling. I spot the door handle to a closet I've never seen before.

"How will we get in?" I grip onto my panic button. Lisa slaps my hand away and frowns. "Be careful!" she warns. "I already wedged this door open, so you need to help me nudge it wider."

Lisa takes the lead by slipping her arm through the tiny gap between the door and the frame supporting it. Sianne and I copy her actions.

"Three... two," Lisa counts. "One... push!"

We groan as we force the door open, just enough so that it swings on its own. I almost cheer triumphantly until I remember why I'm opening it in the first place.

I brace myself for what I'm about to see and slowly tilt my chin upwards to look inside the closet. Instantly, the nausea returns.

There are dozens of dolls, all lined up next to each other. They're of different sizes, heights, hairstyles, races.

I try to be rational and tell myself that these are just ordinary dolls and not humans like me. I'm so desperate to justify what I'm seeing that I ignore the fact that these dolls are made in a style that is an exact replica of the professor's.

"How do you know they were ever human?" I try to mask the horror in my voice.

"I don't," Lisa says. "But he hasn't painted a positive picture of himself, has he? Now that you've met Sianne, the odds of these dolls once being human are probably a lot higher, huh?"

I turn my back on the closet of deactivated dolls and hold my panic button.

"Now for the real question," Lisa drawls. "What are we going to do about this? I think I have an idea. Maybe you can get Gabby to help us out? She seems rebellious enough. Do you think you can do that, Ella?"

I stare at the button, Lisa's words distant.

"Ella?" Lisa repeats, but I don't listen to her. I feel like I'm possessed by another entity. Without giving myself a second to process the consequences, I press the button.

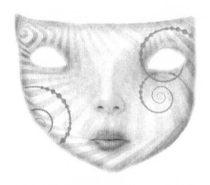

CHAPTER TEN

FINISHED

What did you do that for?" Lisa screams.

"I need him to explain to me!" I clench my jaw. "I need to hear this from *him*!"

Lisa growls and grabs Sianne by the hand. The pair scuttles into the colonnade of boxes.

The professor doesn't delay. The attic door bursts open, and he stands frazzled at the doorway. "Ella!"

"Down here!" I wave. I sense a moment of relief from the professor when he spots me, but that is quickly replaced with intrigue when he sees the closet door open. The floorboards creak when he walks towards me.

"Ella," he begins slowly. "What is the meaning of this?"

I point at the dolls, my finger trembling. "Who are they?"

"They're dolls." He kneels by my side. "But they're not special like you. I've always liked making dolls. You knew that." He stands and reaches for a doll with bright blue hair and pink eyes. She's wearing a costume shaped like a butterfly. He smiles at her fondly and brings her to my eyelevel. "This was the first doll I ever painted. Gorgeous, isn't she?"

I inspect her, half-expecting her face to come to life. "She is. So she was never a human like me?"

"Never." He places her back on the shelf. "Why would you think something like that? You have to tell me what you're doing here."

"Who is my mother?" I demand. "Tell me, right now. What was my mother's name? What was she like?"

The professor sighs and takes off his glasses to rub his eyes. "Why do you do this to me, Ella?" He returns to his kneeling position and scratches his chin. "If you must know, her name was Amber-Rose. She lived in the country, several hours from here in a beautiful cottage that had three horses, two dogs, and daisies aplenty. She looked a lot like you and had your kind heart. She was stubborn—a bit like you, I suppose—and loved her animals more than she loved humans. I liked Amber-Rose..." His voice trails off.

I stick my chin out, a lump forming in my throat. His information is conveniently detailed—the makings of a glorious lie. "And how did you know my mother?"

The professor hesitates, opening his mouth several times before seemingly changing his mind. "I used to offer my services as a gardener, and sometimes she would call on me."

"And is she still alive?"

"Ella, my dear," the professor says softly. "Although you do not age, the rest of the world does. You need to remember that, even though you may possess the body of a twelve-year-old girl, you are in reality, a lot older."

"How much older?" I fight the urge to cry.

"It doesn't matter!" the professor suddenly shouts, his demeanor vastly different. "This is why I turned you into a doll—to protect you from all these lousy human emotions! You used to be so happy when it was just you and I! But now you're acting like you did when you were human—always crying and complaining!"

My jaw drops. The professor notices my mortified expression and immediately lowers his voice, frantically apologizing. I shake my head and back away, slinking into the darkness.

"Ella! Please come back!"

"Go away!" I run into the tower of boxes. "Deactivate me! Do it if I'm such a nuisance!"

"I would never deactivate you, Ella," the professor says sheepishly, dropping to all fours. "I didn't mean what I said. I'm so sorry."

I slump into a corner and block my ears. "Go away!" I scream, squeezing my eyes tightly shut. I don't need to hear his spurious words. When he doesn't respond, I crawl out of the shadows and glance around the room. "I mean it! You... you better be gone! You hear?"

The closet door is closed, and the professor is nowhere to be seen. I pick at my fingernails, a little stunned by his sudden obedience. The professor never leaves me mid-tantrum because he always feels the need to calm the situation.

Lisa emerges from the box tower, one eyebrow raised and her lips curled into a crazed snarl. "Bravo!" She claps her hands in a slow, sarcastic kind of way. She doesn't stop until she crouches down to glare at me. "You've doomed us all. I hope you know that."

"How?" I clear my throat to ease the shake in my voice.

Lisa scoffs, like she can't believe I asked such a ridiculous question. "Now that he knows you're suspicious, we're *finished*! Consider this the last time I ever tell you anything. You're on your own." She turns on her heel and leaves me in silence.

I click my fingers together and stare at the blank canvas ahead of me. Lisa is right.

I'm on my own.

CHAPTER ELEVEN

STALKER

So, maybe, I'm not as alone as I'd like to be.

Sianne has decided to take over my chest. And I mean *take over*. I found her five minutes ago, sitting on my bed cross-legged and meditating. For some bizarre reason, she even found toilet paper and threw it around my room.

Sianne *actually* teepeed the chest.

"Excuse me?" I tiptoe closer to the bed to grab her attention.

"Hummm…" she chants, her eyes closed and her nose upturned.

I groan, too annoyed to be polite. I shake the hinge where her knee should be, and her eyes spring open. She screams dramatically, her fingers suddenly bent like claws.

"Don't *do* that! I was in the Sahara Desert!" She yells, her beautiful posture now slumped. "You don't just pull people out of the Sahara Desert! I'm grounding you!"

"Well, for starters, I'm sorry for ruining your Imagination Time. I know how frustrating that can be. And secondly, I'm not your daughter, so you can't ground me. And thirdly, I'm locked in an attic, so I don't think grounding me will be satisfying."

"Cocklewuff!" Sianne uncurls her legs, ripping the toilet paper that hangs by the bed into shreds. "Ungrateful child! Ungrateful dancing dolly!"

I gently place my hand on Sianne's to stop her from tearing the toilet paper. "Sianne, please stop messing up my room."

She stares at me, her eyes practically bugging out their sockets. She lowers her hands and rests them in her lap, pursing her lips. She looks like a cat that's been sprung doing something naughty.

"I've stopped…" She says slowly.

"Good." I mimic her tone. "Now, Sianne, could you please tell me who you are?"

"Your mother," she replies glumly.

"But you're not." I sit down next to her. "I'd know if you were. Even though I don't have my memories, I'd feel that mother-daughter bond thing. But I don't feel anything for you."

"Nothing?" Sianne asks, deliberately making her lower lip quiver.

"Maybe frustration," I reply honestly, straightening out my tutu to avoid eye contact. "How much of your past life do you remember?"

"Most of it." She wiggles her finger around my nose. "All of it, actually. Bah-humbug. Stupid Christmas. Gah." She suddenly clasps her hands over her ears. "I know *all* about my past! But my brain won't keep it together! I'm not mad! It's when I became a doll! Fix my brain! Make it stop!"

"I don't know how!" I yelp, panicked when Sianne drops to the ground and scratches at her forehead. "What are you doing?"

"Getting the madness out!" She shrieks, furiously clawing at the plastic. "It has to come out!"

"Please stop!" I grab her wrists. She twists so that her feet are by her head, writhing messily as she tries to hit her head with them. "You're a doll, Sianne! You'll break if you carry on like this!"

"Breaking means I can escape! That's what my brother said!"

I pause, wondering which statement I should question. "Who is your brother?"

"Daniel. You know, the professor. Dumb dolly." Sianne suddenly stops scratching at her head. Instead, she gasps and crawls backwards into the corner. "I wasn't supposed to tell you. Are your memories flooding back? Please say no!"

"You're the professor's sister?" I clarify, jumping over my bed to chase Sianne who is crawling from one corner to another. The stupid toilet paper keeps getting in the way, and I have to slash through it to get to her.

"Say your memories aren't flooding back!" She screams, rocking next to my mirror.

"They're not coming back," I say calmly, raising my hands as if to surrender. "Why did you tell me you're my mother?"

"Isn't it obvious?" She sniffs, wiping away real tears. "It's to put you off the scent! You can't know what's happening!"

"But I *don't* know what's happening!" I wade through the toilet paper until I'm standing over her. "Did we know each other in our human form?"

"Of course we did!" She snaps, curling into a tiny ball. "We all knew each other! The professor, you, me, Lisa, Gabby... Well, maybe not Gabby...."

I shudder. The idea of knowing Lisa as a human is upsetting. I can't imagine us once being friends.

"I lie a lot. Most of us dolls do," Sianne adds. "Our brains snap. I wasn't *really* locked in that box for long, not long at all. Hmm. Or *was* I?"

Sianne starts to chant nonsensically, whistling and popping her mouth.

"Sianne," I say slowly, carefully phrasing my next question, "why hasn't *my* brain 'snapped' like yours or Lisa's?"

Sianne rolls her eyes. "Let's just say the professor takes care of you. He'd never let *yours* snap. Also, you haven't been a doll for as long as you think. You have this weird set-up with Daniel. Weird, weird, Black Beard's beard. Said don't look, but oh, you peered!"

I shake my head to clear it. "And he sent you to make me believe you were my mother?"

"Yep. He thought it would make you happy. You're happy, right? Well, to distract you, too."

"Distract me from what?"

Sianne points behind my back. "That."

I struggle to see in the darkness, but it's the professor sneaking into the attic. He's carrying something into the lab. An odd-shaped bag? But bags don't wear frilly dresses or sandals. Bags don't have dark skin and full lips. Bags definitely don't have limp arms and legs.

Bags are definitely not Libby.

CHAPTER TWELVE
REVELATION

Who're you?" a voice asked from behind him.
I don't know why, but the first thing I do is rush straight to my recorder. I press down on the button and speak quickly, my words running into one another.

"Recorder, the professor just took Libby into his lab. She wasn't moving or breathing. I don't know what he's done to her. I have to tell Gabby so we can escape!" I hit the stop button and run.

I don't even remember crawling through the mousehole and rushing downstairs. The only thing I could think of was getting to Gabby.

I found her sleeping angelically in the painfully bland bedroom. I scramble up the sheet hanging by her bed and crawl onto her chest.

"Gabby? Gabby! It's important! Wake up!"

She doesn't even flinch.

"Gabby?" I'd be worried, but she's definitely breathing—I keep rising when she inhales. "The professor killed Libby! He's taking her to the lab! Wake up!"

My voice is quiet compared to a human's, but I'm yelling as loudly as I can. Surely, she should start to stir. I climb up to her face and push her eyelid open, which only *splats* closed again.

I glance at her bedside table, wondering whether turning on her lamp might wake her. It's only when I jump onto it that I notice an opened pack of sleeping pills and a glass of water beside her bed. Of course. I have no chance of waking her now…

I can't help but naturally duck for cover behind the lamp when the light switch by the door clicks and illuminates the room.

Gabby doesn't even respond to the professor, who stands in the doorway, masked in shadow.

"What do you think you're doing, Ella?" I've never heard his voice this deep before.

I don't take my eyes off him. Who knows what he's capable of?

"I'm leaving, professor," I say, my voice shrill and unthreatening. "I need to protect Gabby. We need to get away from you."

The professor turns off the light. He walks towards me, his slow steps matching his chuckle.

I freeze, not sure where to run. He grabs me and shakes his head.

"Now I have to wipe your memories," he huffs, automatically stroking my hair. Condescendingly, Gabby called it. "I already have so much work, as it is. Yes, I'll only wipe the last fifteen minutes. That should do."

CHAPTER THIRTEEN

THE MUSIC IN MY MIND

I never want to stop dancing. Never. Aerial, split leap, pique, pirouette. Repeat at double speed.

I don't care that my ankle twists when I land or that my underarms crack when I raise them above my head. I'm dancing too hard, and it's wrecking my body, but I need the distraction–this one thing that brings me overwhelming joy.

Aerial, split leap, pique, pirouette, and repeat at double speed...

Is this real? Am *I* even real? What if I'm stuck in some absurd dream? I don't know who or what I am anymore. I can't even bear to look at myself in the mirror because I keep expecting to see somebody else.

Aerial, split leap, pique, pirouette, and repeat at double speed...

I'm losing my mind and I don't know who to trust anymore. Maybe, that's why I want to keep leaping–to protect myself from my world that's crumbling beneath me.

Aerial, split leap, pique, pirouette, and repeat at double speed...

I've never spun so quickly. No matter how well I spot, the room becomes a nauseating blur, and my joints complain, squeaking and creaking with each movement.

Pirouette, pirouette, pirouette, pirouette... *crack*.

My leg collapses, and the hinge in my knee snaps. I stop spinning immediately, but can't control my fall. I stumble backwards, hopping on the one leg still attached to me, and scramble to hold onto something to keep me from tumbling off the table. I'm not so lucky. I fall–forever, it seems–until the dust-ridden floor slams into my back. My waist separates from my leg, splitting me in two.

I'm in two halves...

I'm... *broken*. My worst nightmare has come true. What if I can't be repaired? I'll forever be trapped; unable to move, unable to *dance*. I try to sit up when–

—my vision is blurred. I can't discern anything–I'm trapped in green, swampy water. It's bubbling like a fizzy drink about to explode, but I manage to make out the dark edges of my hands pushing against something unseen. Why can't I move? I can't move forward, up, down... anywhere.

That's not the worst part. I can't breathe...

I scramble, thrashing violently and involuntarily as I instinctively gasp for air, only to choke on the thick liquid.

Everything grows darker, and my body weakens. It's a hard feeling to describe, but it's like my brain is leaving it, trying to protect me from my impending, torturous demise.

I need–

"—*HELP!*" I gasp for air when the murky water is replaced with the attic.

Remnants of my watery grave still flash before me, but I can breathe. Or rather, don't need to. I hit the attic floor with the back of my arms instead, assuring myself that I'm back in my doll body, then lie back and stare at the ceiling. Just what in the world has happened?

"You called?" I recognize the voice immediately and strain to sit up, but Sianne only tenderly caresses my forehead and motions for me to stay down. "I can put you back together."

"No!" I rub my head. "I was in green water. I know I was! What was that?"

Sianne has brushed her hair and taken off her lab coat to reveal a pretty frilled dress with a petticoat. She looks a lot more approachable and friendly now, but madness still sparkles in those huge aqua eyes. She's carrying a tube of superglue, which she lowers beside me.

"Sianne? What happened?"

"You're not supposed to break," Sianne says calmly, picking up my comatose legs and readjusting them so that they can fit into my hips again. When she is satisfied with the placement, she unscrews the superglue lid. "When you break, you return to the place where you were as a human, which was that green water you probably thought you were drowning in. That's why the professor is always so freaked about you breaking. He doesn't want you to go back to that place."

"What do you mean, I return to the place where I was human?"

Sianne purses her lips and shakes her head, holding my legs in place to allow the glue to set. "I've said too much. Next question." She smiles gently, before flinching like she's forgotten something.

"What? What is it!"

"Three-million, four-hundred and seventy-eight thousand, one-hundred and ninety two!" Sianne yells triumphantly and cackles like a witch. "I remember! 3-4-7-8-1-9-2! That's the code to my lab! You have to remember! You have to tell the professor! I'll be free! *FREE!*"

"3-4-7-8-1-9-2? Okay, okay, got it! But free from what?"

She lowers her voice and darts her eyes, grabbing me by the shoulders to shake me. "The more you remember, the less you forget! Daniel is helping you! Little dolly forgot last night..." Sianne delicately removes her fingers from my shoulders while she stares at something I can't see. "The didgem-hoppers are watching me again..." She bobs her head. "Next question."

I prop my hands behind my head so that I can crane my neck to see her. "Fine." I think for a moment, concerned that Sianne only has a designated timeframe before she reverts to a less lucid state. "What do you mean I forgot last night?"

"*I* remember," Sianne says with a conceited flare to her tone. "I made lots of noise to make the professor come out of his lab. I hid, but he saw you were gone, so he chased you downstairs. My wonderful brother… it's my job to tell him when you've run away… naughty, sly dollies."

I fidget while she speaks, itching for more information. "So—"

"—you only get two questions," she interrupts, putting her finger to my lips. "Now we can talk about politics and religion."

"*Two* questions?" I snort. "What are you? A cheap genie?"

"If I tell you any more, *your* brain might snap from information overload! Snap, snap, snap!"

"Do you understand how infuriating these answers are? It's like that TV show, *Lost*. Each answer only leaves you with more questions." I wriggle my legs to see if they move. When they do, Sianne leans her bodyweight onto my legs and shakes her head furiously.

"Stop! The glue hasn't set yet!"

"Okay, okay." I roll my eyes and sigh, even though I can't feel the oxygen stream through my lungs. There's no point in me chatting her up–apparently I've already reached my question quota for the day.

Sianne eases up on the pressure on my legs and curls her feet under her dress. "So," she says awkwardly, "why were you dancing like that? Hasn't the professor told you to be careful not to break?"

"Oh, so now it's your turn to ask questions?" My response is spiteful, but totally whooshes over Sianne's head. She continues to sit contritely with wide eyes and curved lips, so I force myself to answer. "He freaked out about me doing anything because he said that I'd break, but he never said what would happen if I did. I just thought I'd…"

"Die?" Sianne finishes.

"Yeah." I shake my head. "I mean, no. I don't know! I was just so confused, with meeting you and seeing those other dolls…" I groan and tug at loose strands of my hair. "It doesn't matter!"

Sianne carefully pulls her hands from my legs, watching them intently to ensure they are secure. "It's okay to be confused," she says. "Life is very confusing. The fact that we breathe air, create music, and fall in love is all very nonsensical, but it doesn't mean we need to analyze it. Just enjoy the moment, because it's gone once you know you're in it." She puts her hands in her lap and smiles, seemingly proud of her speech.

Maybe Sianne has a point. Before Lisa arrived, I enjoyed life—even when it wasn't spectacular. Since she tried to break me, she has been a vacuum of misery, sucking me into her deluded world. I desperately want to scramble back into the life I was happy with, but I'm not happy there anymore, either. I haven't found the world I belong to yet.

"What on earth is your accent? It's nothing like mine!" I force a chuckle. Even though my laughter is fake, it makes me feel a little better.

Sianne shrugs. "A little bit of this and a little bit of that." She smiles and mumbles something under her breath. "I have to go." She scratches at her neck. "Lisa will wonder where I am. I pretend I'm her minion. I'm actually the professor's minion. Funny word. *Minion.*"

Sianne reluctantly slinks away into the tower of boxes.

"Wait!" I shout, too scared to move in case the glue hasn't set. "Sianne? Wait!" The outline of her body stands still in the darkness, watching me from afar.

Great. I now have two crazy dolls I have to be on the lookout for.

Cautiously, I sit up, squeaking loudly. I touch my knee and am relieved when my hand doesn't stick—at least, that means the glue has dried. I stand, but not as steadily as I'd hoped. My knee slips out of joint, nearly knocking me off my feet again. I frantically grab my leg and force it back where it should be and remain hunched over, grasping for balance. It might be a while before I can dance again… hey, it might be a while before I can even *walk* again.

My movements are akin to the Tin Man–stilted and awkward. Every step I take is balanced out with a one-minute rest.

When people swore on TV, I'd block my ears because I knew it was rude and inappropriate, but right now, I feel the urge to use a highly unnecessary profanity.

It takes me all night to reach my treasure chest, but there's no way in the world I can pull myself into it. I still need time to heal.

Gently lowering myself to the ground, I rest my back against the treasure chest. These pathetic legs! Well, at least I'm not split in two anymore–I mean, *that* would've been a hindrance.

I attempt to close my eyes, but cringe when they creak. Good grief. I really *am* the Tin Man. Soon I'll be asking Gabby for the oil can.

The only thing I can do is sleep and hope to wake up miraculously healed. Either that, or be endlessly relegated to the pits of imagination time. The recorder rests on the other side of the treasure chest, so I could probably make that walk.

I lean against the chest to pull myself up, and lumber towards my recorder, keeping one hand on the chest and the other on my leg.

My eyebrows furrow when I make out the machine. It's in the dark, but something is wrong with it; I just can't quite work out what.

"No," I whimper when I trip on bits of plastic scattered across the dust-covered floor. I hobble closer and collapse when I see the irreparable damage. My recorder is completely smashed, like someone has dropped it from a great height and proceeded to stomp on it. "Professor! Professor!" I scream, unable to tear my gaze from the remains of my recorder.

The familiar hurried footsteps sound outside before the professor bursts through the door, his hair sticking up like he has been half-electrocuted. It must be the middle of the night, because he is dressed in blue-checked pajamas.

I point at my recorder, horrified that he hasn't noticed the plastic massacre.

"Imagination time!" I shriek. "It's gone! Forever! Professor, you *have* to fix it! *Please!*"

He towers over me, staring at the remains. He removes his glasses to rub his eyes and shrugs, then turns his back, opens the attic door, and steps outside.

"Professor? What are you doing? Are you going to get some glue? We have some in here!"

"No," he says from the doorway, his face masked in shadow.

I hesitate. "Tomorrow, then?"

"I broke your recorder," he says simply, putting his glasses back on.

I don't have a heart, but I feel it shatter.

"Why?" I ask, my voice meek.

"Because I like to listen to your imagination time while you sleep. But instead of hearing Ella's Rescue Squad, I heard a disturbing message from you."

I gape at him. "*Really?* I don't remember this. What did it say?"

"I'm not telling you." His tone is polite, as always, but his words cut deep. "I don't know why you left a message like that. Perhaps Lisa is getting to you. I need to find her and put an end to her madness."

I've had enough. First, I broke in half. Then, my faux-mother appears with incoherent answers. And now, *this?* I feel like I'm going crazy! I curl my hands into fists and raise my voice.

"Professor, I've had a really rough day, okay? Nothing's making sense! Have you ever listened to a song stuck on replay? Had the same tune, lyrics, and beat slamming into your mind over and over until you feel like all your thoughts are muddled? This is how today feels. So why don't you just treat me like a normal person and tell me the truth?"

The professor hesitates, tapping the doorknob vehemently. "Because you need to forget your past," he says, slamming the door.

I dart my eyes to and from the recorder. What past?

CHAPTER FOURTEEN

BYE-BYE SWEETIE PIE

I really don't know how I feel about you calling my grandfather evil. Yeah, he's controlling, but come on!" Gabby brushes my hair with one of her doll's brushes and twists it into two symmetrical knots. I sit on the attic floor and stare into the mirror Gabby brought in. I look *so* fake. Like *devastatingly* fake. No human has bulging eyes like mine and a twig neck. The professor's attempt at making me beautiful has only turned me into an aberration.

"He smashed my recorder! He knew how much it meant to me! And did he apologize?"

"Well, yeah, okay, that was pretty nasty," Gabby mumbles. "But nasty doesn't equate to evil."

"Then how do you explain him turning his own sister into a doll? What kind of person *does* that?"

"But maybe there's more to it? You said she was pretty crazy?" She pins a clip into my hair. "I'm just sitting on the fence, here."

I roll my eyes. "Yeah. Crazy is one word to describe it. Mental institute crazy. I can barely bring myself to even speak to her. She kept whispering strange numbers." *3-4-7-8-1-9-2*. I can't seem to forget them.

Gabby laughs, grabbing the hairspray. "Aunt Sianne used to do that. She died a few years ago, but Dad always talks about her. He's convinced she's still alive, but–why are you looking at me like that?"

My mouth hangs open. "She is still alive," my voice breaks. "That's the doll that's hidden away! The professor's sister is your Aunt Sianne!"

Gabby frowns and shakes her head. "No way. Because that would mean–"

"–you're related to a crazy doll. Let's hope you don't inherit the madness!"

We burst into hysterical laughter, before remembering that we're not supposed to.

"Do you ever get the feeling we might be related?" I ask softly, hoping I haven't said anything out of line.

"All the time." Gabby's smile is as frank as is contagious. "You said Sianne kept saying she was your mother. If she *was*, wouldn't that make us, like, second cousins or something?"

"I've always wanted a cousin!" I giggle when Gabby picks me up and squeezes tightly. "Maybe we could pretend to be cousins? Would that be weird? It'd be nice to at least *act* like I have family…"

"That's not weird." Gabby adjusts the clip in my hair. "Let's just say we're cousins."

"Agreed." I sigh deeply, squirming in Gabby's grip.

"What's wrong?" She lowers me to the floor.

"I can't get Sianne off my mind. Not only is it creepy that she's tried to convince me she was my mother, but she admitted that it's her *job* to spy on me! She says the professor put her up to it, but I don't know, she seems to say one thing and mean another…"

Gabby shrugs. "Maybe she turned herself into a doll for funsies?"

"No," I say. "No way in the world. *He* did that to her, and he did it so he knew what I was doing… of every minute, of every day…"

"But you don't know that for sure, do you?"

We flinch when a paintbrush crashes to the floor and rolls towards us. Gabby and I gaze up at the two dolls standing on the table. One is shorter than the other and twitching. The other holds my gaze with a formidable stare.

Gabby jumps up and enters some kind of karate position. "You stay away from my cousin, psychotic goth doll!"

Lisa sniggers and waves half a tissue above her head. "I surrender, I surrender. Look, I'm not evil. Sianne told me how our brains kinda go weird when we're turned into dolls. Isn't that right, Sianne?"

Sianne points at her head and twists her finger. "Crazy like a coconut."

"Anyway, I couldn't help but overhear your conversation." Lisa's smug smile is really starting to grate on me.

"Ella, press your panic button!" Gabby instructs.

"You know you'd be silly to," Lisa warns. "Look, I get the whole 'it's-awkward-now-that-you're-all-family' scenario that's going on, but in reality, you just have to accept that the professor is the bad guy, here. I wasn't going to tell you anything else, but *I'd* be the bad dolly if I didn't. I have one last shred of evidence to demonstrate. How long ago was the ballet?"

"Three days," I say, but it feels like a lifetime ago.

"Right. Three days. And how many days do you think it takes to kidnap a girl and turn her into a doll?"

"Five!" Sianne interrupts. She pauses and taps her chest. "I mean, seven!"

Lisa rolls her eyes and motions for Sianne to hush. "It's a trick question," she says quietly. "It takes less than an hour."

I swear time stops. It's like I can't even hear anything anymore. Gabby and I remain frozen, hoping against all odds that Lisa isn't insinuating what we think she is.

"What are you talking about?" I finally say, shuffling towards Gabby's ankle and cuddling it.

Lisa checks her nails, now painted electric blue. I don't know where she keeps finding these shades. "I stumbled across something you're not going to like. The professor seems uncomfortable creating dolls in the attic now, so I thought I'd check his office. I got the feeling you might recognize her." Lisa steps sideways and turns her head to the left. "You can come out, now."

A doll emerges from behind one of the pencil holders. Her beautiful dark skin matches her cocoa eyes and hair. Her strapless dress has bright red and green stripes, with sandals to match.

"The professor calls her Libby." Lisa presses her lips together. "Recognize her?"

Gabby goes weak at the knees. She stumbles towards Lisa and Libby, leaning against the table for balance. "Oh my God. *How?*"

Libby politely curtsies and offers her hand to shake. "Hello! Lovely to meet you. I've been told by the professor that we've met before. I vaguely remember going to school with you and a party with dodgems, but not much else, I'm afraid."

"Why is this happening?" Gabby shouts at Lisa. "You're lying! This may look like Libby, but there's no evidence!"

Libby puts her hands over her ears. "With all due respect, miss, the professor explained that I was broken, so he protected me."

"How?" Gabby asks. "How are you 'broken'?"

"He said I was sick," Libby says matter-of-factly and smiles, her teeth unnaturally white.

Gabby covers her mouth with her hand and closes her eyes, dry heaving. Lisa looks irritatingly smug, tapping her foot to an imaginary beat.

"Sick, eh?" Lisa speaks in such a sly and condescending tone that I want to slap her. "Aren't *you* sick, Gabby? I could be wrong… but the recent pattern would indicate…"

Gabby shoots Lisa a disgusted look and grasps her. She

squeezes Lisa tightly, as if she has every intention to crush her waist. Despite Gabby's wide eyes and snarl, Lisa remains surprisingly serene.

"Don't think he won't do it," Lisa says. "He turned his sister into a doll, so what makes you think you're safe? And Ella here isn't even sick, yet she's been a doll for years."

I'm not sick? I want to question it, but I don't want to give Lisa the satisfaction. Instead, I puff out my chest and try to convince myself that the professor really is the good guy. But there's nothing I can think of that depicts him in a positive light.

Gabby looks at me for reassurance, but I can't give her that. I'm compelled to believe Lisa.

"So… you really think that my grandfather will turn me into a doll because I'm sick?" Gabby asks, her eyebrows puckering when Lisa nods.

"I can guarantee it," Lisa says, seemingly enjoying Gabby's discomfort.

"It's true," Sianne chimes in, oblivious to the gloom and doom. "We're all sick in some way. You don't *have* to be diseased to be turned into a doll. You might be depressed, like Lisa."

I've never seen Lisa look so vulnerable. She whirls over to Sianne. "*What?* How do you know that? Tell me!"

"You're not depressed now, are you?" Sianne asks.

"No!" Lisa snaps. "But I'm suspicious! Tell me what you know! Was I depressed?"

Sianne stuffs the ends of her hair into her mouth and chews. "We're all here for a reason," she says, her voice muffled. "We're all broken."

We remain silent, lost in our thoughts.

"Then I can't stay here," Gabby whispers, snapping us out of our respective trances.

"It doesn't seem so bad!" Libby says, her optimism reminiscent to my previous outlook on life. "The professor says I would've surely died, but now I'm free to be healthy and happy!"

Gabby's eyes dart from Libby to Lisa to Sianne to me. "Ella? What's being a doll like? *Really* like?"

I contemplate a pros and cons list. For an undetermined length of time, I've been confined to a dingy attic where I spent the majority of my time watching TV and longing to go outside. The professor controlled me to the extent that I forgot what it was like to even make a decision. I constantly made up storylines of my life as a human, wondering where I went and who my family was. I longed to taste juicy fruits and delectable desserts. I wanted to know what it was like to breathe, to feel, to *live*. Beyond all else, I always wondered what my life would've been if I had never become a doll.

I cringe before the words even escape my mouth. "Run, Gabby."

Gabby turns to Lisa who nods in agreement.

"We'll come with you," Lisa says solemnly. "I thought the treatment could be reversed, but I've done some more sleuthing. Once you're a doll, that's it. There's no more hope for me to change back. The least I can do is stop you from becoming one."

"We'll be with you until the end." I stroke my new cousin's ankle.

Gabby whimpers with each touch, until she bends over and slips me in her jeans pocket. She picks up Lisa and Libby and reluctantly slides them into the pockets next to me, then reaches for Sianne who squeals and hurries behind the pencil-holder.

"You have to come with us!" Gabby says, her entire body shaking. It's like being in a dry Jacuzzi.

"I *can't!*" Sianne clenches her jaw. "Daniel told me to stay!"

"What?" Gabby asks. "You're in on this? Ella was right?"

"I came here to keep you off the track, that's all. That's my job. I must do my job. Jobs are important." Sianne tilts her head to the side and widens her eyes. "I must help my brother. Family is life."

"Then why have you teamed up with Lisa?" I ask.

Sianne's eyes click when she blinks. "BECAUSE I'M CRAZY!"

"Forget it," Lisa snaps, tapping impatiently on Gabby's jeans. "We haven't got time for this."

The four of us jolt when the stairs outside creak. It's the professor. Gabby freezes, staring at the door like a rabbit caught in headlights.

"In here!" Sianne bounces up and down, screaming as loudly as she can. "Professor! They're escaping! Hurry!"

Lisa tugs on Gabby's shirt and hits her side. "He'll be here any second! Go-go-go!"

"Oh!" Libby squeals and claps her hands. "This is exciting! Where are we going?"

Gabby doesn't need to answer. I know exactly where she's going.

Except, once she's at the window we climbed through the first day we met, she has more trouble forcing it open—I'm guessing she's probably a lot weaker now.

"Where do you plan on going?" Lisa asks when Gabby sits on the windowsill.

"Home," Gabby grunts. She looks over her shoulder. "Aunt Sianne! Shut up!"

Sianne ignores her and continues to jump up and down like the loon she is. "Daniel! She's out of the window! Quick!"

"How far away is your home?" I ask.

"About a ten-minute drive." Gabby grabs the drainpipe and begins her descent. "I need to tell my parents about Grandpa."

"But what if they're in on it?" Lisa huffs, dangling her arms from Gabby's pocket like a ragdoll.

Gabby stops mid-climb. "What do you mean?"

"Well, I think there are a few contributing factors at play. The fact your parents sent you to live with your nutty grandfather is a bit of an indicator that they know what he does. But maybe I'm reading too much into it," Lisa adds innocently.

Gabby snorts, taking careless step down the drainpipe. "That doesn't me—"

There's a *crack* as the drainpipe bends under Gabby's weight. She loses her grip and we all scream as we plummet. I close my eyes—I don't want to break again. She lands briefly on her feet before she collapses to the ground, writhing on her back as she nurses her ankle.

"It's broken! I've broken it!"

Lisa jumps from Gabby's pocket and clings onto her tummy, frantically trying to calm her down. "Are you hurt anywhere else? Gabby? Gabby, listen! Do you hurt anywhere else?"

"My foot!" she screams, rocking back and forth.

Sianne appears at the windowsill, her tiny body barely visible against the panes. She gasps and points to us. "Professor! Get in here! Gabby's broken! She's a broken girl!"

"It's probably just a sprain!" Lisa shouts over the screams, desperately trying to remain calm. "I heard a sprain can hurt more than a fracture. You have to get up, Gab! The professor will hear you!" Gabby's face turns red as she wails even louder. Lisa springs forward and slaps Gabby on the nose. "Gabby! Pain is fleeting! Turning into a doll is forever! What's it going to be?"

Almost instantly, Gabby's sobs subside. She sits up and winces when she puts pressure on her foot, which is already swelling. "Ow!"

"Is your other foot okay?" Lisa asks, bounding towards Gabby's feet to check. Gabby puts pressure on her other foot and doesn't flinch.

"The other foot's fine," Gabby sniffs, taking jagged breaths.

Lisa slips back into Gabby's pocket and lowers her voice. "Then you can hop. Let's go! And stick to the bushes! We don't want your neighbors to see you hobbling around. They'll take you straight back to the professor!"

"Daniel!" Sianne squeals from overhead. "You're here! *Finally*! Look out the window!"

"*RUN!*" I scream.

Gabby nods determinedly and limps towards the main road, groaning with each step. She rests against a tree three houses down from the professor's. We can't hear Sianne anymore, but I'm stunned that the professor hasn't caught up to us yet, despite his bad hip. Part of me wonders whether Sianne was just pretending to speak to him... after all, she's convinced that didgem-hoppers exist--whatever *they* are.

I look back at the house, having never seen it from this angle. We are apparently on the end of a cul-de-sac. I never knew about the rocking chair on the light blue front porch, or the well-kept lawn with sprinklers lightly flicking water.

It's only from examining the house that it suddenly hits me. What have I done? Sure, I'm saving Gabby from a life as a doll that will accomplish nothing, but isn't that better than no life at all? Maybe it wouldn't be so bad. And I'm sure I can convince the professor not to deactivate Lisa!

And what am I going to do in the real world, anyway? I'm a *doll!* It's not like I can go to school or get a job. My only real home was with the professor, I mean, *my grandfather,* safe to do whatever I pleased far away from the dangers of reality.

"We have to go back!" I squirm to get out of Gabby's tight pocket.

"What?" Lisa and Gabby say in unison, albeit in two very different tones.

"Come on!" I plead. "What were we thinking? This is insane! Gabby, you're going to die out here! And what's going to happen to us, huh?"

"Probably nothing in the next half hour," Lisa says. "We're going to Gabby's parents. And if they turn out to be in on it, we'll run to the police."

"And then what?" If I were capable of hyperventilating, I surely would be, by now. "The police take the professor away? Then Gabby's parents? Then she's sent to a foster home? To while away her last *days* there? And what happens to us? Either we pretend to be dolls and are thrown away or we come clean and are sent to a laboratory for observation!"

Lisa doesn't answer.

"We'll play it by ear once I reach my parents." Gabby closes her eyes and leans her head against the tree. "Ooh, I'm so *sick* of these headaches!"

"Do you need to sit down and rest?" I pat Gabby's hip, the only place I can reach.

"I wish," she puffs. "I haven't even left the street, and it feels like I've run a marathon."

"We need to leave this area, and then maybe we can call a cab," Lisa suggests, bumping against Gabby's leg. "Time to move it, girl. The professor can still see us from here!"

I glare at Lisa. "Don't push her! She's sick!"

"Desperate measures," Lisa hisses, hitting Gabby's leg with surprising force. "Come on!"

Gabby nods and obeys Lisa, hobbling down the street and wiping away tears.

When we reach the end of the road, Gabby throws herself to the ground so that she's sitting like a mermaid on a rock. "I'm done," she pants. "I'm so done."

"No!" Lisa shrieks. "You can't give up!"

"I'm done," Gabby repeats. She closes her eyes and lays down.

Lisa squeezes out of Gabby's pocket and pokes her nose. "Hey! Wake up! We're almost there!"

"Leave her alone!" I yell, crawling onto Gabby's lap. "You know what, Lisa? I've had it up to *here* with your nonsense! Look what you've gotten us into!"

This is the first time I've seen Lisa look genuinely surprised. "*Me?* What did *I* do?"

"The weather is awfully nice today, isn't it?" Libby interjects quietly, maintaining her place in Gabby's pocket.

"You know what you did!" Libby and her ill attempt to mollify the situation can go stuff it. "You've caused nothing but trouble! I was happy until you arrived! You ruined everything!"

"I think you'll find that the professor ruined everything!" Lisa bites out, raising her shoulders like a stooped werewolf.

"Guys?" Libby chips in.

"I was a broken human!" I cry. "I don't know how or why, but the professor did what he thought would be best for his family!"

"Guys?" Libby says again, her voice slightly higher this time.

"He's evil! It's his own sick experiment!" Lisa retorts.

"*HEY!*" Libby shouts. "Look!"

I do—and a chill runs through me. Blood is trickling from Gabby's nose and staining her pale lips. I rush towards her face and prod her, frantically trying to wake her up. "Hey? Hey, Gab? Gabby? Wake up. Gabby, *wake up*. *WAKE UP!*" I'm getting more and more hysterical with each syllable. More useless. "We need a human to help!" There's no way we'll reach the professor in time. I glance at the house beside us and leap up. "Libby, Lisa! Follow me!"

I collect tiny bits of rocks and sticks off the ground and throw them at the front door and windows.

"What are we doing?" Libby asks, her throws timid and unsure.

"We have to get their attention. If they come out, they'll see Gabby and will call an ambulance. *HEY! WE NEED HELP! COME ON!*"

"Do we yell, too?" Libby whispers to Lisa, who solemnly nods.

Together, we yell and toss rocks at the house. Our throws are weak, but it's the best we can do.

When the door unlatches, we drop the rocks and jump back into Gabby's pocket.

"What the bleedin' hell?" an older woman barks when the door swings open. She scans the area, but doesn't notice Gabby partly hidden behind one of the shrubs.

"Oh, no," I whisper. From Gabby's pocket, I yell at the top of my lungs, "HELP! A GIRL IS DYING! HERE!"

The woman wears a floral dress and a stern expression. She takes a longer stride so she's standing in the center of the lawn. All she has to do is turn to her left and she'll see us.

She looks to her right...

Please look left...

She looks to the front...

Please look left...

And finally...

"Oh! Frank! Frank, there's a young child out here! Bring the phone!" The lady hurries towards us and instantly checks Gabby's pulse. She says a quick prayer and sweeps Gabby's hair to the side. "Frank! Where are you? This girl isn't breathing!"

My chest tightens and a squeak escapes my throat. Lisa glances at me from the corner of her eye, but we remain frozen in Gabby's pocket.

"What's all this about?" Frank, a thin and balding man, appears at the doorway with the phone pressed against his ear. He gasps when he sees Gabby in his wife's arms and shuffles over. "This is... yes, an ambulance. 38 Pinnacle Drive. We have a young girl, about ten or twelve, she's collapsed in our front yard. She has blood streaming from her nose. No, we don't know who she is."

"Yes, we do!" the woman snaps. "She belongs to Daniel at the end of the street!"

"Oh," Frank's voice quivers. "Yes, we do know her. She's a neighbor. Will you be here soon?" There's a beat while we wait for a response. "Really? Oh, good! Thank you!" He hangs up the phone and crouches next to his wife. "They're only minutes away! How did you find her?"

"I heard yelling." The woman's eyes well up. "She's so young. You need to get Daniel before the ambulance comes. He lives in the house with the blue porch. Go!"

"Okay." Frank kisses his wife on the cheek. "I love you."

"I love you, too." She squeezes his hand, then swipes at a runaway tear.

There's a twinge of... I suppose it must be jealousy in my gut.

There was this spark, an invisible light that shone through when they touched. I guess they call it a true love.

Another thing I can never experience.

We wait in silence, the distant cries of the ambulance a harsh reminder of our reality.

CHAPTER FIFTEEN

MERRY CHRISTMAS

Wake up!"

I'm rudely awoken by a soft pillow slamming into my stomach. I grunt as if I'm in pain, but I barely felt it.

Gabby is beaming, clutching her pillow as if it were a shield.

"You little monster!" I reach for my own pillow and smack it over her head. She giggles hysterically, just like when I pin her down and tickle her torturously.

She dodges my next swing and bolts out of my bedroom, slamming the door behind her to slow me down.

I chase after her, a mad smile spreading across my face. We hurry downstairs and skid to a halt when our parents exchange confused looks in the living room.

They sit by the fireplace with mugs of hot chocolate in their hands. The Christmas tree winks at us as Michael Bublé plays lightly in the background.

"Why aren't my girls dressed yet?" Grandpa mock-growls,

heading to the kitchen to prepare our hot chocolates. "Because I do believe Santa visited us last night."

Gabby and I gasp and race towards our stockings neatly hung on the mantel.

"Mine's bigger!" I brag.

"Because it's probably full of coal!" Gabby retorts, scrambling through her stocking.

"Yeah, and? Do you know how expensive coal is?"

I pull out my first present–a Lea Doll. Lea Dolls are collectable dancing dolls, each with their own background story, dance style preference, and fashion sense. I have Brightly–the too cool for school dancer with bright red hair and an affinity for rap music. I squeal and shove the box into Gabby's face.

"So what?" She pulls out a matching box. "I got Starful–the Spanish ballet chica!"

My jaw hangs open with jealousy. "Swap?"

"No way!" Gabby cuddles her box. "But we'll definitely share them?"

"Well, duh!" I grin.

The remaining presents include less exciting items, such as underpants, flashlights, drink bottles, dresses, books, and a sled for Gabby and me to ride together.

"Could we play with the sled now?" Gabby begs, rolling up her pajama sleeves.

"There are no hills around!" Mom protests, followed by a chuckle and a noisy slurp of her drink. "We're leaving for the mountains in two days, you two can use it then."

"I guess we have our dolls to play with until then." Gabby pouts, poking at a Christmas tree ornament as Uncle Greg and Aunt Fay begin carving into the turkey in the kitchen. In unison, Gabby, Grandpa, and my parents glance into the kitchen.

"Are we ready to feel fat and tired?" Uncle Greg inquires, dishing the eagerly anticipated meal onto our plates.

We all murmur excitedly and seat ourselves at the dining table. Gabby and I fight over who gets to sit next to Grandpa, until he calmly pulls our chairs so that we end up on either side of him.

Grandpa's the best.

"Shall we toast?" My father asks, raising his sparkling water in the air. I don't know why, but I've never been able to see his face. It's just a black hole covering his features. The same goes for Uncle Greg and Aunt Fay. Their bodies and hair are clear, but they are without noses, eyes, and mouths. It's probably because I don't remember what they really look like, and my imagination can't create a face out of thin air.

I gaze at my mother. Her features are large and doll-like, and her head bobbles on her thin neck.

I grimly turn to look at Gabby, her glowing face slowly morphing into a pale, gaunt substitute.

The color drains from my perfect scene, until our warm Christmas is completely replaced with white walls, a beeping machine, and a doctor at the foot of Gabby's bed.

CHAPTER SIXTEEN

LIAR, LIAR

The doctor is young—I'm guessing he's in his thirties. His dark hair is swept to the side, and his coat looks a little too big for him.

"Prognosis?" The professor asks, rubbing his face.

"She overexerted herself." The doctor makes a show of checking his chart. "With her condition, there's no way she should be doing anything physical."

"We went to the ballet a few days ago." The professor's voice trembles, and I feel like a heel. "Should I not have taken her?" Should I not have encouraged her to go?

"No, that would have been fine," the doctor reassures. "I'm talking about running, climbing. She has a sprained ankle, and you said your neighbors found her on their lawn?" The professor nods so the doctor continues. "Excuse me if this offends you, but do you have cause to believe she was running away from home?"

"No," the professor croaks, his shoulders shaking when he inhales. "No, everything was fine."

"We see a lot of this behavior in our epidemic patients." The doctor tucks his chart underneath his arm and tries to smile supportively. "Especially in the younger ones. They try to run from their problems–literally–and only end up here. Towards the end, they start having vivid hallucinations. One young boy was convinced he was a human trapped in a dog's body."

The professor raises his eyebrows and glances at me. I remain as still as possible, but I refused to let go of Gabby when the paramedics let her in. I held on for dear life and let the professor explain that I was Gabby's doll and that I made her feel better when she was sick.

The professor slid Libby and Lisa into his coat pocket before anyone saw them. They squirm slightly now, but they should know better than to make a scene in public.

"Do all epidemic patients imagine they're trapped inside another being?" The professor queries, keeping his eyes locked on mine.

The doctor shrugs, oblivious to my disgusted expression. "There are some reports of patients believing that they are inanimate objects, such as kitchen appliances, bikes, dolls." He motions at me. "It's sad, really. Gabby hasn't experienced any such symptoms, has she?"

"Not yet," the professor says. "So, will she be discharged soon?"

"Under normal circumstances, I would suggest that she stay the night, but considering the timeframe we are operating against, I would recommend gathering friends and family and making her as comfortable as possible at home. She's stable, so I'm confident enough to release her. Just avoid physical activities," he warns, then checks his beeper. "Oh, I have to go. I have been waiting for this consult. Just buzz the nurse if you need anything. She'll be in shortly with the forms. Take care, okay?"

The professor hunches and puts his face in his hands as the doctor steps out. He sighs when I noisily scramble out of the gap between Gabby's arm and side that I'm pinned between.

"Let me guess." I yank down my tutu that has risen to my neck. "You're going to take Gabby home and turn her into a doll just like Libby?"

"Don't start, Ella!" the professor growls. "I'm not in the mood."

"I'm not working around your schedule anymore!" I yell, pointing my finger at him.

"I'm the only one who can save her," he whispers harshly, nervous eyes darting at the door. "Get back into your position. A nurse might walk in."

"Turning someone into a doll doesn't save them." He just doesn't understand, and oh, I'm so fed up with him playing God!

He leans in closer—so close, I see how large his pores are. And funny, I never noticed how light or bloodshot his eyes are. "*You know nothing*," he hisses.

I scoff and settle back into Gabby's arms. "You can turn me back into a human, can't you?"

The professor doesn't dignify this with a response. He merely reaches for the magazine on Gabby's bedside table and flicks through it.

"I know you can!" I press, trying to find a way to catch him out on a lie. "Lisa said the process was reversible!"

"It's not. And Lisa knows that. Nice to see you've been lying to me about seeing her, though."

Like he should be talking. "Why are you keeping me prisoner? Change me back!"

"You won't want to go back!" the professor barks, his lips quivering. "Please, trust me, Ella."

I lie silently, unsure how to respond. It's only when I look up at my motionless, sleeping little cousin that I speak. "Please don't turn Gabby into a doll."

The professor looks up from his magazine. "Sorry?"

"Please don't turn Gabby into a doll," I repeat dutifully. "It's horrible being a doll."

The professor... Daniel... sighs and cleans his glasses with the handkerchief he keeps tucked in the sleeve of his lab coat. "You really don't know what I'm about, do you?"

"Of course I don't. You never tell me anything."

"Of course, he doesn't!" Lisa's voice is muffled, but she finally manages to poke her head from the professor's pocket.

The professor pushes her back down. "Shut up, Lisa," he speaks as if he's lost the will to live. "You don't know what I do, either. You don't remember everything."

"I remember enough!" Lisa snarls, poking her head from his pocket again. "Like how I was in this hospital before I woke up in your dingy little attic as a doll! I *bet* my human body is around here somewhere!"

It's as if someone just hovered a lightbulb over my head. "Lisa... You meant to bring us in here..."

"Yeah," Lisa says, her tone unapologetic.

"You knew Gabby's condition was bad. You convinced her... *you convinced me*... to run away, and you knew her body wouldn't be able to handle it. You knew we would be brought to the hospital."

"Yep." She smiles smugly. "And I have to say, I'm annoyed you didn't believe that Sianne was your mother. You're not as dumb as I thought. She can't be trusted either, you know. She's working with your precious professor."

Thump. It's distant, but I feel a heartbeat in my chest again. Only this time, it's a beat of frustration and anger. My hands clench into fists.

The professor rolls his eyes and pulls Lisa from his pocket, gripping her around her waist. "Pray tell, Lisa." His tone drips with disdain. "How do you plan to escape from me and roam the hospital? Your body isn't here, you know." He pauses. "You're far from it."

Lisa squints and gnashes her teeth. "Liar!" Without warning, she pulls a safety pin from her shirt and jabs the professor's thumb with it. It's enough to make him yelp and release his grip, allowing Lisa to drop to the floor and sprint for the door.

The professor stands to chase her, but she's already gone. His jaw hangs open while he stares after her. "Oh *crap*."

"I think," I say, sure that I'm mirroring his expression. "You're allowed to say something much worse than that."

"She has been *nothing* but trouble!" He clenches his jaw and swipes his arm at something imaginary. "I've only ever tried to help her!"

"What do we do?" I wrap my hand around Gabby's finger.

"We can only hope someone finds her and smashes her in a moment of weakness," the professor says darkly. He calmly resumes his seat and finds his place in the magazine.

"Don't say that!" I stumble across the hospital bed, shocked by how springy it is. This has to be what being on the moon feels like. "We have to find Lisa!"

"You're not going anywhere." The professor turns the page of his magazine. "I'm done with her. If someone finds her, it won't trace back to me. I'm sick of cleaning up her mess. Like I said, she's beyond repair."

"What does that *mean*?" I strangle the air with my hands. "Professor, I'm so confused! You're not painting a pretty picture of yourself! You look like the psychopath who turns little girls into dolls for the fun of it! Heck, I'm not even sick and..." I trail off when the professor's head shoots up.

"You're not even sick?" he repeats slowly. "Where did you get that idea?"

"Lisa said..." I begin, although now I'm starting to feel stupid.

"Did we not just experience firsthand that Lisa is a liar and a manipulator?" The professor smirks and then starts to chuckle, almost hysterically. "Not sick! Ha!"

"Why is that funny?" I fold my arms defensively.

"Ah, Ella." He wipes away a tear. "If only you knew."

I don't bother to ask him what he means. I know he won't tell me. Settling back into Gabby's arms, I lie quietly, listening to officious voices mumbling in the hallway and the professor leafing through the magazine too fast to actually read something.

Libby pokes her head from the professor's coat pocket and stretches her arms. She yawns and glances around the room, batting her eyes. "What'd I miss?"

CHAPTER SEVENTEEN

MADDOX

The professor's blinks are heavy and slow. He keeps jerking awake when his head flops to his chest, but he won't be able to keep it up for much longer.

He mumbles something incoherent, so I don't respond. His head rolls back onto the headrest, his eyes closed. This time, he doesn't flinch awake.

Perfect.

I squeeze out of Gabby's arms and lower myself onto the hospital floor, pleasantly surprised by how clean it appears. I swear the dust in the attic is bigger than me.

"Libby!" I tug on the professor's coat that's hanging by the chair leg. "Libby! Are you awake?"

Libby pops her head out of the professor's pocket like an excited puppy. "Ella!"

"Hey." I raise a finger to my lips to hush her. "Do you want to come and find Lisa with me? She ran off and the professor doesn't want to look for her."

Libby nods and awkwardly climbs from his pocket, falling onto her head. She lies twisted on the ground, looking up at me apologetically.

"I'm assuming you were never a cheerleader." I offer my hand to help her stand. She accepts it and dusts herself off.

"So, how are we going to get around without the humans seeing us?"

I glare at Libby, offended by the way she phrased the question. "We're humans, too. We're just humans trapped in dolls."

Libby shrugs. "Yeah, okay. So what are we going to do?"

I pause and stare into the hallway, hoping that a miracle will present itself.

"Hey! What about that?" Libby points at a wheelchair, folded and leaning against the wall.

I grin. Of course. We just have to wait for someone to wheel by and we'll jump on.

"Great idea!" I grab her hand and tiptoe towards the doorway. A peek from the side reveals a person in a wheelchair slowly making their way down the hall. "When I tug on your arm, we're going to jump in the bottom of that wheelchair."

"The part where they put their bags and stuff beneath the seat?" Libby clarifies, nudging me out of the way so she can see the target.

"Yeah." I push her behind me. "Okay, it's coming. Are you ready?"

"Yes!"

"Steady?"

"Yes!"

"G–wait. Wait, not yet." I psych myself, waiting for the wheelchair to hurry up. "Okay! GO!"

Libby and I dive into the back of the wheelchair, bouncing on the leather base. The wheelchair seems to move a lot faster now that we're in it.

"Do you have any idea where Lisa might be?" Libby whispers, sitting as still as possible to avoid detection.

"No!" I scan the passing rooms. "But we have to try."

"I don't understand why, though." Libby runs her fingers through her hair, combing the frizzy parts. "You don't like her. You say she's a liar and stuff, so why do you care?"

"Because I don't leave anyone behind," I say quietly, sinking into the material when the wheelchair comes to a halt. The rider shakily stands and slumps onto the bed, pained moans escaping with each movement. When they settle and the moans cease, Libby and I scramble out and hide beneath the bed to get our bearings. All these hospital rooms look the same.

"We're lost, aren't we?" Libby sighs and starts fidgeting with her dress.

"No one is ever lost," I say encouragingly. "It's just time to figure out where to go next."

"So we *are* lost?"

"Well, yeah." I kick the bed wheel. "Where would Lisa go to find her human body?"

Libby shrugs. "The morgue?"

I freeze. "That's downstairs, isn't it?"

"I don't know."

"We'll never get downstairs undetected!"

"Maybe because it's not meant to be?" Libby scratches at her nose even though I'm confident she doesn't have an itch. She's sickeningly well-adjusted.

I go to say something, but I'm interrupted by a young boy in a hospital gown sobbing in the hallway. He's holding something close to his chest and stroking it. A woman—his mother, maybe—speaks to him tenderly and leads him into the room across from us.

"But I only just found her!" he cries.

"Shh… Settle down, Maddox!"

I can't hear anymore, so I pull on Libby's arm and sneak out from underneath the bed. Scoping the hallway from the doorframe reveals some nurses up ahead, but they're not looking in this direction. We leap along, vulnerable and visible. It feels like an eternity to reach the room on the opposite side. When we get there, Libby and I crouch behind a plastic plant by the door.

"She was just someone's doll you found," the woman says reassuringly, sitting by Maddox's bed.

"No!" he screeches. "She spoke to me! She was real! She came in here, and then the stupid cleaner broke her! She won't speak anymore!"

"Who?" The woman strokes the boy's dark hair.

"The doll!" Maddox yells. "The doll the cleaner broke! Why aren't you listening to me? Look!"

I want to be sick when he lifts the object that he kept close to his heart. It's Lisa, but her face is smashed and her body is mangled. She hangs limply in the boy's hand, beyond repair.

I can't look anymore. I cover my eyes and bury my head in Libby's shoulder. "She's a broken doll." I sob. "She just... doesn't exist anymore."

"But everything exists," Libby insists. "Energy doesn't just disappear."

"We defy science, Libby," I say firmly, lifting my head from her shoulder. "I think the rules are a little different with us."

The woman awkwardly snatches Lisa from Maddox's grip and tosses her into the bin by his bed. He screams and shouts obscenities at her.

"I'm not going to take this nonsense!" the woman says, standing to leave the room.

"You're going to leave me here?" Maddox shrieks. "I'm sick!"

"You had a routine operation to get your appendix out! Now stop this! I need to speak to your nurse." The woman storms past us, leaving Maddox to have a tantrum in his bed.

"Let's get out of here," I whisper to Libby.

"How? I don't remember where Gabby's room was. Do you?"

I shake my head. "We'll wing it. We found Lisa, didn't we? I'm sure we can find our way back."

"Who's talking?" Maddox shoots up in his bed. Wow, he has good hearing.

I keep quiet behind the plant, but Libby seems to have other ideas. She steps forward and waves. "Well hello, there!"

I stay hidden, silent, *mortified*.

Maddox gasps and jumps from his bed, crouching down to speak with Libby. "Did you come to find your friend? She broke!"

Libby smiles sweetly and nods. "I overheard what happened to Lisa. Do you think you could do me a favor?"

He nods emphatically. "Anything! I feel so bad for what happened! The cleaner's mop thing went straight over her... and then there was this noise... and some kind of green mist left the doll's face... and then she stopped talking."

I frown and step out from behind the plant. "Green mist? Did she manage to say anything?"

"Oh!" Maddox says. "A dancing doll! Cute. Um, she was asking me something like...um, if I had seen a human that looked like her. When I didn't know anything, she got frustrated and didn't look where she was going. Walked straight into that electronic mop thing. And yeah, a green mist just appeared from her broken face and floated out the window."

Oh my God. Maybe Libby was right. Maybe Lisa still exists. She's still alive... "Maddox, right? Could you please carry us back to our friend's room?"

"Of course! Yeah!" He scoops us up and shuffles out into the hall, wincing with each step. "Which room?"

I try to follow the door numbers without turning my head or eyes, not that I actually know Gabby's.

"This one!" I announce when I recognize the bright glare of the professor's lab coat.

Maddox turns into our room, halting when the professor pins him to the wall with his glare.

"Who are you?" The professor's still in his chair, dark rings beneath his eyes.

"I brought your dolls back," Maddox says, shifting uncomfortably. "I found them in my room."

The professor stands and angles his head so his eyes are looking over his glasses. "Give them to me," he says, his voice uncharacteristically deep.

Maddox suddenly tightens his grip around us. He gulps, but stands his ground.

"Child," the professor speaks slowly, exposing his palm. "Walk to me and hand me the dolls."

"It's okay, Maddox." I pet his hand. "The professor won't hurt you."

Maddox lowers his head to whisper to me. "I'm not worried about me. I'm worried about what he'll do to you."

"*WHAT?*" the professor snaps, taking large strides to reach our little hero. He tugs on the boy's arms, desperate for Maddox to release us. "Give them to me!"

"Professor, stop!" I squeal.

"Not until he gives you over!"

Maddox reluctantly passes us to the professor and nurses the part of his arm where the professor grabbed him. "I'm telling!" He sobs, hurrying out of the room.

"What did you do that for?" I yell, as the professor lowers Libby and me onto the bed.

"Because he's mental," Gabby's tired voice says. Surprised, I swing over.

"You're awake!" I squeal, bounding towards her to cuddle in. She giggles, weakly, but brings me close. Oh, I wish she really were my cousin. The lie made me feel bonded to her, like we had something special. Of course, even though we're not family by blood, we're sisters by nature. And in a way, that's even better.

"Yeah." Her voice is croaky, but still optimistic. "Where have you been? I've been so worried!"

"Lisa ran away. She lied to us, about my mother, everything. I still couldn't help myself–I had to find her."

"And did you?" the professor snaps, his body stiff and his expression hard.

I nod. "The cleaner broke her. She's... she's gone."

The professor's reaction startles me. He slams the magazine onto the bedside table and paces on the floor. "I didn't *really* mean I wanted someone to break her! We have to get home! *Now*! Gabby, come on!"

Gabby nods at her hospital bed. "I'm kind of indisposed at the moment!"

"No, you're not!" The professor grabs the wheelchair pressed up against the wall. It unfolds, and he maneuvers it over. "Quick, get in. You're fine to go home. The doctor said so."

"I'm not ready!" Gabby's eyes water. "Just let me rest! Please!"

"Gabby, she's going to ruin everything! I need to get you home so I can save you before it's too late!" A vein appears near the side of the professor's forehead. "You have to trust me! Get in the wheelchair!"

Gabby turns to me for reassurance, although I'm not too sure how to give it to her. Is there anyone left we *can* trust?

I link my hands around her finger to show my support, and she nods firmly. At least, we're still together. She slowly crawls out of bed, holding onto the professor for support, and drops into the wheelchair.

"Boy. That was hard," she wheezes. "I'm not fond of this whole being sick and weak thing."

I jump onto Gabby's lap and wave at Libby to follow. She jumps–almost missing–and lands next to me. We freeze while the professor wheels us out of the glaringly white hospital and into the parking lot.

He picks Gabby up and slides her into the backseat so she can lie and rest. Libby and I hold onto one another as we rock back and forth while the professor speeds down the road. He doesn't stop for traffic lights and doesn't slow down rounding the corners. Whatever happened to Lisa...

—A jolt of electricity pierces my skin, my organs, my eyes...

Everything's blurry... everything's dark... everything hurts so much.

I can't breathe. I'm drowning again. Water seeps into my mouth, my nostrils, my lungs.

A dark figure with its arms crossed watches me with a smile on its face... It's... It's Lisa.

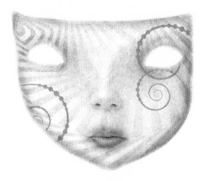

CHAPTER EIGHTEEN

THE LAB

I don't mean to scream when we pull up in the driveway. My daydream was just so real.

"Ella?" The professor turns in his seat. "Are you okay?"

Gabby tickles my shoulder supportively as I hyperventilate.

"I was drowning," I gasp. "I mean, it was a dream... oh, but it *couldn't* have been! It was too real!"

"It *was* real," the professor mutters, undoing his seatbelt and slamming the door behind him. He opens the rear door and scoops Gabby into his arms. "Libby, Ella—hold on to Gabby."

We do—and bounce on her belly as he jogs through the house and up the stairs. I swallow another scream. Why is he so determined to get to the attic?

When he kicks open the creaky door and lowers Gabby to the floor, a sense of relief washes over me along with resentment. It's dusty, it's dirty, it's my prison more than anything else. But it's home.

Libby squeals with delight when the professor picks her up and places her into my treasure chest. She runs straight to my comb resting beside the mirror and begins to brush out the tangles in her hair.

Really? There's Zen–and then, there's Libby.

The professor hurries back and cups Gabby's cheek. "Stay here, please. Don't come into the lab."

"Okay," Gabby says. She rests her eyes, too tired and weak to protest.

The professor grabs the keys from the back pocket of his slacks and unlocks the door to his lab. I follow him and stand by his feet, a little unsure about how I feel about finally seeing his lair.

"Ella," he says softly. "I don't know how you're going to react when you see this place."

I look up at him, twining my fingers together.

"Please trust me," he says. As if he'd been ever so trustworthy. "It's going to be hard."

My chest feels tight, that strange distant heartbeat making itself known again. I manage to give the professor a shaky thumbs-up, and he lets us in.

I can't see much without the light on. I always imagined the floors to be like the ones at the hospital, but instead they match the attic–worn floorboards and peeling, brown wallpaper. It's nowhere near as professional as I thought it would be. Towering over me are counters, Bunsen burners, and large tubes or tanks.

He walks in slowly, and I follow. It's very dark, but the professor won't turn on the light. Instead, he stands frozen in the center of the lab, staring at a corner.

I know what he's looking at. It's a tall figure–just under six human feet–typing on one of the many keyboards. Water drips from their waist-long hair, and their dark clothing sticks to their body.

The figure stops typing and slowly turns to face us. The glow of the computer screen allows me to see one side of her face, while the other is masked in shadow.

Mascara runs down her cheeks and settles by her nose. Her eyes aren't aqua or purple—they're a light brown. She has small lines beneath her eyes, and her eyebrows look thick and unkempt. When she sweeps her damp fringe behind her ear, fresh scars on her wrist zigzag along her skin.

"It's nice to be human again." Lisa's voice is even huskier than what it was as a doll. She steps forward, but her knees nearly go out from under her. She quickly leans on the counter for support, knocking over a few beakers. It's only when the beakers smash on the floor that I realize there's a lot of glass that's already been shattered. Where did all of these shards come from? "Although, I suppose you were right about one thing. My body *wasn't* at the hospital. Sorry for dragging you down there for no reason."

"Are your human memories returning?" the professor asks cautiously. "Do you understand why I did this to you?"

"Of course I remember!" She rolls her eyes, still bent over on the counter. I can't get over how different she looks. Her face is a lot harsher, especially because of the way her skin crinkles when she frowns. "I mean, sort of. It's coming back slowly. But just because I remember everything doesn't mean I condone it! It's sick, Daniel! You need to release Ella!"

"You have no right to speak on Ella's behalf," the professor lowers his voice and steps towards Lisa, glass crunching beneath his shoes. "What I do isn't *sick*. I'm doing the right thing."

Lisa scoffs. "I spent a lot of time trying to work out what you did. I found my way into this lab and I studied your notes. What an idiotic design—*smash the doll, and the consciousness returns to the body. Real smart, genius.*" She begins to pant, like she's out of breath, even though she just stands there.

"You're still weak, Lisa." The professor raises his hands in an effort to calm her. "You weren't supposed to return to your human body yet. It's still healing."

"I had to get out!" Lisa shrieks, slouching over the bench even more. "I didn't understand what had happened to me! Don't you see your experiment was failing? Ella said she started hurting, started *crying*! You overloaded the system because you kept adding too many dolls! We all started remembering and feeling things because you don't know how to run your own lab!"

"Mistakes happen," the professor says calmly. "But I can assure you whenever Ella began to experience pain or remember the accident, I would alter her subconscious to suppress the memories."

"Professor?" I look up at him and bare my palms, physically pleading for answers. "What accident? What's going on?"

He shakes his head. "Not now, Ella."

"By all means, continue to lie to her," Lisa says harshly, grunting as she forces herself to stand without the help of the counter.

The professor flicks the light switch and the fixtures come on, exposing the human-sized tubes in the corner. There are five of them, but one is empty and has a gaping hole in the middle. The other tubes are filled with murky water and... and... *EWW...* shadowy figures curled up like fetuses.

"What are *those*?"

"I'll tell you in a minute," the professor shushes me, his tone impatient. "Lisa, please come and sit down with me. We'll grab a cup of tea and talk about this like adults."

"That's the thing, though." Lisa grabs a micro spatula and twiddles it in her hands. "I'm *not* an adult. I'm a kid."

Without any warning, she charges the professor, clutching the spatula like a knife. She's tall—about the professor's height—and he has trouble blocking and restraining her.

I scream helplessly and take cover underneath one of the stools. If only I could help! If only I weren't a doll!

"Lisa!" the professor shouts, holding her by the wrists. She squirms out of his grip and tries to pierce his skin with the micro spatula. "Calm down! You're being silly!"

"Shut up!" she yells, pushing him against the countertop. He stumbles and lands on his back, groaning and wincing in pain when he tries to move.

"Lisa…" This time, his voice is agonized, and my heart breaks a little.

"Stay down, old man!" Lisa rummages through one of the drawers. She pulls out a rope and tests it by wrapping it around her own wrist. Satisfied, she bends over to tie the professor's hands. "And if you get up, I'll knock you out."

The professor rolls his eyes. "Real life isn't like the movies. If you think you can knock me out for an hour so you can do whatever it is you want to do, prepare to be disappointed. If I'm unconscious for that long, I'd have severe brain damage."

"Well, maybe that's what you deserve." Lisa fishes out duct tape from the same drawer and slaps a piece over the professor's mouth. "Now where's that dancing doll?"

I whimper involuntarily and stay hidden beneath the stool, curling into a small ball to conceal the bright colors of my leotard. Imagining Lisa as a doll is nowhere near as scary as what she is now.

"Ella?" Lisa coos, flipping the micro spatula in her hand like a baton, not even flinching when the sharp end slices her skin. "Come out, come out, Daniel's precious."

She drops to the ground and rests her cheek on the floor so she's at my eyelevel. That reveals me instantly, and she grins, exaggeratedly motioning for me to join her. I shake my head.

"Ella, you're not running anywhere, just so you know. I tied up your beloved professor to show you something. If you know the truth, you can do with it what you will. Does that sound fair?"

I hesitate. Lisa is so good at manipulating me–she always makes out like everything she says and does is in my best interest. Still, I need to find out how she became human again. I *have* to.

I reluctantly step forward out of the shadows and fidget with my fingernails. Lisa sits up and crosses her gangly legs, placing the micro spatula by her side. She smiles, this time more pleasantly, and straightens my tutu.

"Thank you," I whisper, too terrified to speak any louder.

"Don't be scared, sweetie. I remember everything now, and it's worse than I thought. We're not letting the professor turn Gabby into a doll, and you're going to get the chance to become human again. Would you like that?"

I look up at Lisa with wide eyes and shrug. I'm getting the feeling being human isn't everything it's cracked up to be. "I just want everything to go back to normal…"

"Oh." Lisa's eyebrows arch, and her mouth forms a perfect 'O'. She shakes her head and continues with more enthusiasm. "Good answer. Everything *will* be back to normal."

We stare at each other in silence for a moment, and I get the strong urge to run away. I lift my foot to run, but I'm frozen in fear, allowing Lisa to determine my destiny.

It happens in slow motion, but I do nothing. Lisa stands, her shadow engulfing every shred of hope, of *choice*.

She raises her shoe above my head, and it hovers for a moment.

"It'll only hurt for a second," she says.

The pain lasts a lot longer than a second. I'm blinded by the view of the shoe crushing into my face and suffocated by the weight behind it. I hear myself bend and break and feel my body separate from my limbs.

Once the pain fades, all I can see is green.

CHAPTER NINETEEN

REBORN

My eyes sting when they flutter open. Misty green liquid cradles me. I try to breathe, but only choke when it enters my sinuses.

The sound is exactly like the underwater documentaries I watched–heavy with pressure.

I bounce helplessly and frantically scratch at the glass. When that doesn't work, I clench my fists and pound away, but that doesn't work either. I'm so weak, I can't even move my legs to kick against the glass. Everything is slow in water. Slow and pointless.

"Close your eyes!" A muffled voice yells. Confused, I make out a dark figure outside the tube holding a... I think that's a crowbar...

I try not to panic and shield my face from the incoming force. The crowbar smashes into the glass, and the water rushes through the jagged hole, taking me along with it. I land heavily on my back and roll onto my side, spluttering for air. I gulp the sweet taste of oxygen when the water absconds from my lungs–I didn't know breathing felt so freeing.

There's a strange cramp in my abdomen that seems to spread with each second. It hurts, but I ignore it the best I can because I have more important things to worry about.

My vision is blurry–and exceedingly painful, like I've never used my eyes before–and my clothes feel big and heavy. I instinctively go to stand, but Lisa crouches next to me and shakes her head. "Don't move," she says softly. "You're not strong enough."

"Huh?" I frown when I register my own voice. It's different. It doesn't have the melodic tone of a singer. Instead it's croaky, nasally, and... *old*. "What just happened?"

Lisa inhales shakily and caresses my face. I pull away, unsettled by her sweet disposition.

"Do you have any of your human memories?" Her hair is slowly drying and curling at the tips, and she's taken off her wet duds and replaced them with one of the professor's spare coats.

I move my hand into a more comfortable position and flinch when a piece of glass sticks into my palm. I slowly remove it, startled by the crimson liquid trickling along my skin. I'm bleeding...

"I don't remember anything..." I say, smearing the blood across my hand.

"Okay, I was afraid of that," Lisa mutters, heading towards one of the computers. She types something into the computer and looks at me. "Ella?"

I don't respond. I'm too busy feeling the joints in my fingers move and getting used to my chest rising when I breathe. I feel everything–my heart, my teeth, my throat–everything, except my legs. Everything else moves when I want it to, but not them.

"Why can't I walk?" Ugh! That horrible croaking that passes for my voice... And my legs. I hit them, but they're numb. "Something's wrong with them."

Lisa inhales loudly again. "This should jog your memories. I'm just warning you–you're not going to like it."

"Why not?" I ask, but I don't hear a response. Within moments, I am once again smothered by darkness.

CHAPTER TWENTY

WHEN IT BEGAN

Somehow, **Daniel was handsomer once we were married.** As soon as he said 'I do', his face grew brighter. His eyes shone, his cheeks flushed, and his lips glistened.

He was absolutely perfect.

I've never met anyone who smiled as much as Daniel. He was always happy–quiet, but gloriously happy.

But how could he not be? He had just started working from home, far away from the politics that were the bane of his office. We threw in our savings and built a laboratory in the attic so he could create a cure for every disease.

Life was perfect. I had the sweetest two-year old who was exceptionally bright and I got the feeling he'd take after his father when he grew up. He was currently staying with my mother while Daniel and I honeymooned. Jason was born out of wedlock and with our busy schedules, Daniel and I had only now just decided to get married and take a well-deserved vacation. It would be agony to leave my baby boy behind, but I was assured we had both earned a delayed wedding and a week away to ourselves.

My mother said I was a fool for supporting Daniel. Her words always echoed in my head, "so long as there are cures, there will be disease, no matter what. Nature gives and nature takes."

Don't get me wrong–my mother loved Daniel; she just didn't *believe* in him. No one believed in Daniel. Just me.

"Sweetheart, we're going to lose our reservations." I pushed on the laboratory door. As expected, he was rushing from beaker to beaker, tweaking water levels and testing the electric charges.

He was still dressed in his wedding suit, albeit the tie was loosened and the shirt untucked.

"One moment, dear," he said, pausing briefly to blow me a kiss. "An idea occurred to me during the reception. What if our bodies can't heal whilst we're conscious? As humans, we are indoctrinated into speaking negatively and believing the worst in others. Our bodies can't heal if our mind won't allow it! What if I removed the consciousness so that the body could heal? It's revolutionary!"

"It's madness!" I laugh, joining him so that I can link my arm through his. I stand on tiptoes to gently kiss him on the cheek. "But all the best ideas are mad. Can you do it?"

"Not yet," he mumbles, wrapping his arms around my waist. "But I will! It will require a lot of testing before I make it public. My problem is working out where to *send* the consciousness while the body heals. I don't want to put people into a coma, exactly. They should still be able to live happily and healthily. I'm also working on an injection to help fight diseases in the body! If I combined that with a consciousness transfer, it would ensure fast and effective results!"

"Daniel, do you mean to tell me you were thinking of *that* during our wedding reception?"

"Yes!" He squeezed me all the tighter. "I've always said you're my inspiration!"

I couldn't help but giggle like a schoolgirl when he picked me up and twirled me in the air, just like the boys used to do in dance class.

"I try." I adjusted the straps on my mermaid-green dress. There was no need for me to wear white, after all. "But seriously, you can have a look at this later. We're an hour behind already!"

"My petulant doll." Daniel nuzzled my forehead. "Meet me in the car while I finish this up."

"I bet I could choreograph and learn a whole new dance number for opening night by the time you're done!"

"You're on. What's the date of your debut, again?"

"The third. You know, this could really make my career. A star role in an off-Broadway musical! Do you think you'll leave your experiments at home when we walk the red carpet?"

"Depends on how rich and famous you are…" Daniel poked his tongue out and winked.

I rolled my eyes and puttered down the stairs, careful not to trip on my gown. When I reached the bottom step, I allowed myself a moment to admire the cream carpet, the peach walls, and the violet curtains. I loved my home. It wasn't glamorous or overly big, but it was mine. I could never imagine leaving it. Not for long.

A shortcut through the living room took me into the garage, where I threw myself in the car and cranked up the radio so I could sing along while I waited for Daniel.

I'd never felt so happy. Sure, I was sitting in a dim garage singing to myself, but I honestly didn't care. Not much bothered me, which is why Daniel and I worked.

I'd only sang two and half songs when Daniel joined me in the car—and the singing. He didn't know the words, mind you, but that didn't stop him from belting it out.

We hadn't booked an expensive honeymoon—we just decided to leave the suburbs and spend the week in the countryside an hour from home. Daniel reserved a sweet cottage for us called the Honey-Milk Barn. The photos looked exquisite. Roses lined the path leading to the glass door and daisies sat by the windowsills. The bedroom was a deliberately rustic loft that overlooked the living area with its old-style TV and a cozy couch made for cuddling.

"My throat is getting sore," Daniel said, slowing around a sharp bend in the road.

"Oh no! Are you getting sick?" I felt his forehead with the back of my hand.

"Nah." Daniel chuckled. "It's from singing too much."

"That's because you don't do it from your diaphragm!" I ran my fingers along his sternum. He squealed when I tickled him, trapping my hand between his chin and chest. "Let go!"

"Then stop tickling me!" He playfully batted my hand away, and I conceded defeat. We were probably only forty-five minutes away, but the flurry of packing and the heartbreak of leaving our little guy for the very first time were taking their toll.

The road was deserted and dark. It wasn't usually this dim by eight-thirty, but the trees blocked out what was left of the sunlight. We wound along one of the back roads—the ones that truck drivers usually took so they wouldn't be penalized for driving over their hours. Daniel ensured me it was a quicker route, but I'd felt a tad uneasy. I always liked people around me and knowing my place on the map—but it wasn't until now that I realized that Daniel was all I needed.

"I'm going to rest my eyes for a minute." I yawned, my blinks getting heavy.

Daniel chortled. "Turning into an old married lady, sweetheart?"

I poked him on the arm. "Just tired of putting up with you!"

"I'm sure." He smirked, turning down the volume. "Go on, Ella. I'll wake you when we arrive."

I reached for his free hand and squeezed it. "I love you."

"I love you, more. You're my world," Daniel said, briefly diverting his gaze from the road. When it swung back, a profanity escaped his lips.

Daniel frantically pulled on the wheel and swerved violently to the left to avoid a large deer standing in the middle of the road. The deer escaped unharmed, but the car rolled once, screeched, groaned, and *smashed* into the side of the tree.

And my seatbelt... It didn't keep me in my seat like it was supposed to. In one blurry moment, I was thrown off, the glass pierced my skin, and the road slammed into me for all I was worth.

The ringing in my ear didn't last long, and then, I was deafened by silence. The car lay totaled against the tree, smoke or steam or something floating from the engine and up towards the heavens. I couldn't see Daniel in the car.

My heart fluttered, like it skipped a couple of beats. I tried to run towards the car, and collapsed when I attempted to stand. Nothing hurt, but nothing worked. It didn't make sense. Instinctively, I crawled towards the car, then stopped, distracted by the wetness. Had I been out that long? Did it start raining? I glanced down at the gravel, and my head spun when I realized it wasn't rain that was soaking my body—it was a long trail of blood that smeared the road. *My* blood.

"Daniel?" My voice shook when I reached the car. Dents dotted the doors, and all the windows were shattered. I tugged on the handle, but it wouldn't budge. "Daniel? Sweetie?"

No response. Weakly, I released the handle and slumped to the ground, breathing so quickly, no air actually made it into my system before I choked on a putrid smell... Smoke? Yeah. That was smoke. The car would go up in flames any second.

There was no noise... only the weeping cries that leaked from my mouth.

There was no one around... no one, except the deer that stared at me from the other side of the road. When I acknowledged its gaze, it turned its back on me and bolted into the woods.

CHAPTER TWENTY-ONE

THE ROAD

Ella?" Daniel's voice was urgent. "Gabriella? Gabriella, speak to me!"

Why was it so hard to keep my eyes open? How did he find me? Had I been sleeping for long? I caught glimpses of Daniel–the gash on his head and the dirt on his face.

"What happened?" I push through lips too cold to properly obey me. "Are you okay?"

"I'm fine. I was thrown from the window, but I didn't go far. I found you by the driver's door." He pulled me closer to his body, my blood staining his shirt. The sound of sirens echoed in the distance. It was a sound I always dreaded when I heard it in town, but at this moment the piercing ring was a sign of hope.

"Have I been dreaming?" My voice was slurred and I had no real control of my words. It was like I wasn't in my body. "I had that dream of the ox again. Recurring dreams are just my imagination being lazy."

"Shh, Ella," Daniel said, rocking me like a baby. "Everything will be okay."

"You called me Gabriella?" I pointed out, my eyes rolling to the back of my head. "You only call me that when there's a problem. Is there a problem?"

"You're concussed, my love," he whispered, closing his eyes and gulping on his words. "Your legs aren't working right now, but they will. I promise they will."

"I have to dance next month," I reminded him, my face growing cold. Lucidity was not on the cards right now. "I'm enrolling Jason in dance class, even if he *is* a boy. When he's older, he can be a scientist by day and a dancer by night. He's wonderful, isn't he? He'll be the best of both of us."

Daniel suddenly howled, the way I did when I was giving birth to Jason. His pained cries matched the level of the ambulance and police cars that came to an abrupt halt when they found us huddled in the middle of the road.

"Why are you crying, Daniel?" I asked as the medical team lifted me onto some portable bed thing.

"Because I ruined you!" he sobbed, pacing with his head in his hands.

"Don't be silly! I'm so lucky!" My voice was slow and nonsensical. "I'm the luckiest girl in the world…"

CHAPTER TWENTY-TWO

MY LITTLE BROKEN DOLL

Y ou might walk again," Daniel said reassuringly, stroking my hair. He looked so vulnerable with that bandage wrapped around his head.

I *hated* the hospital. The constant glare, the sanitized smell, the random beeps. No Jason.

"They said I wouldn't." I stared to the side. How could this paralyzed lump of meat and tears ever be enough for him now? I was half a woman, a burden. I couldn't walk, and I couldn't dance. Without dancing, I was nothing. After years of hard work, I would've had my first paid performance next month. It was going in front of casting agents and renowned artists… All a pipe dream, just like chasing my growing son around the neighborhood playground.

Daniel tugged on the sling that his arm was in, struggling with the itchy material. "What if…" He cleared his throat.

"Out with it," I said, my voice dull from lack of sleep and constant crying. "What if what?"

Daniel scratched his nose as his chair tilted against the bed. "What if you were part of my experiment?"

"Which one?"

"The one where I transfer consciousness to another object so that the body can heal!" His eyes filled with enthusiasm, like he'd just split the atom. "We can do it!"

I shook my head. "No. It only works with disease. This is bone and nerve damage."

"It's *worth a shot*, Ella!" Daniel pleaded, his eyes watering. "I hate that I did this to you! What if... what if I put you inside a doll? That way you could still dance? Your body would heal in a... in a tank, yes! You could still do everything you wanted while you waited. You could still *dance!*"

I hesitated, mulling over the repercussions. It wasn't like I had a job or could care for my child. And hey, there was a chance it could actually work!

"There's just one catch," Daniel lowered his voice. "I'd need to wipe your memories, but only temporarily."

I blinked. "Why?"

"Because how can the body heal when you remember what happened to you? The concept is this: if you're happy, then you give positive vibes to your body. You can't know anything about your life except for the things that bring you happiness–like dancing, painting, nature."

"That makes sense..." I said slowly, my chest tightening. Could I really do this? Forget my wedding, my family, my *life?* "How long would you put me in for?"

"We could try a year and see how you do. After one year, I will return your memories, and we'll assess the changes. Then it will be up to you whether you want to return to your human life..." Daniel inhaled nervously. "God, it has to work! I *need* to fix you. I can't live with the guilt."

"Can't I be allowed to remember who *you* are?" I swept his hair behind his ear and wiped away the single tear from his cheek.

He shook his head, pursing his lips to control the sobs. "No. It might trigger everything. As far as you'll know… I'll just be a professor. A crazy professor, secretly in love with a little doll."

"But you'll still be in my life?" I swallowed against my own tears. "You'll never be far?"

"I'll be right there with you. *Every* day. I made a vow, and I intend to keep it."

"But I'll remember what the house looks like!" I reached for the tissue box. "I picked out everything. What if I see our wedding photos? The curtains I put up? The monkey bars we just installed for Jason?"

"I'll keep you in the attic." Daniel looked shocked by his own words. "I mean…yeah, you can live in the attic. I'll make it nice for you, though. You're never there, so nothing should trigger a memory. Plus, you'll be right beside my lab, so I can keep an eye on you."

"You can't clean to save your life. The place will be a mess."

"I'll try. I'll try my hardest!"

"But won't I remember you? You're my husband, Daniel."

"It'll be like amnesia. You'll be comforted by me, and you'll love me, but you won't know who I am in context. But if I expose you to too many ties to our past, like the rest of the house, your memories might come flooding back."

"And what about our son?" My voice cracks. "What about Jason?"

"Your mother can take care of him, or, maybe, Sianne. At least until you get better." Daniel wrapped his good arm around me, allowing me to weep into his shoulder.

"I was going to dance onstage next month." I burrowed into his neck. "It was a sold-out performance."

"You'll dance again." He said firmly. "I'll make sure of that!"

"As a doll?" I laughed, almost hysterically. "Do you really think it could work?"

When Daniel nodded, his head became a vicious blur. "Yes, Ella. This will be revolutionary, and I promise, you won't be gone for long. Jason won't even have the time to miss you. For a short time, you will be my little broken doll."

I leaned back in the bed and squeezed Daniel's hand tightly. "Let's do this."

CHAPTER TWENTY-THREE

THIRTY YEARS

Untie my husband," I say, staring at the professor in the corner.

Lisa's eyebrows raise and her jaw drops. "*Husband?*"

"Yes." I click my fingers impatiently. "Untie him."

Lisa shakes her head. "No way! He's a psychopath! He turned us into dolls!"

"This was my choice. And if I recall correctly, your parents asked Daniel to turn you into a doll. I reverted back to my human form last month when Daniel decided to clean out the tanks. He told me all about you."

Lisa slams her hand on the counter and strides towards me, bending over to meet my gaze. "*What* did you say about my parents?"

"I've gone back and forth from human to doll, human to doll, human to doll many times," I say calmly. "This is probably my fifteenth time, but unfortunately, my memories are erased each time. I do remember Daniel saying something about his good friend Tony…"

"That's my dad." Lisa clenches her jaw. "What about him?"

"Tony was worried about his daughter. She was going through *a phase.* Cutting herself, drinking heavily." I pause and narrow my eyes at Lisa. "You know the drill. Tony's daughter contracted something very bad one day. Something *incurable.* He asked Daniel if he could help his little girl's body heal by transferring her consciousness."

"So you're *in* on this?" Lisa whispers, backing away and leaning against the counter. Her chest rises and falls as she struggles to comprehend the situation.

"Untie my husband," I repeat, managing to pull myself into a sitting position. "He'll be able to tell you if you're cured or not. If you are, you're free to go back to your family." I cringe as I listen to my voice. It gets more grating the more I speak. It sounds like I need to cough up a frog.

I'm actually surprised when Lisa reluctantly steps behind the professor—I mean, *Daniel*—and complies. Maybe it's because I'm an older woman, and she feels obliged to listen. Or maybe she's still in a state of shock. Regardless, I'm getting my way.

"And when you've done that," I say steadily, "retrieve my granddaughter from outside. We will begin the process to turn her into a doll. We don't have a lot of time."

"A lot of time for what?" Lisa flings the ropes to the ground. Daniel rubs his chafed, old-man wrists and stands uneasily. He glares at Lisa and steps around her to the computer.

"Gabby is dying. Once she's in the tank, it will slow down the virus. In time, she will heal. Hurry," I add when Lisa gapes at me. She hops on the spot a moment before briefly disappearing through the door and reentering with Gabby in her arms.

My granddaughter, Jason's daughter, is unconscious. We really are running out of time.

Daniel flicks a switch that turns the bubbles on within one of the empty tanks. He motions for Lisa to join him.

"What are you doing?" She pants, her arms shaking from the weight. Granted, Gabby wouldn't be heavy—but Lisa and I are both weak from not using our bodies.

"Saving her," Daniel replies quietly, untangling cords. He proceeds to plug the end of one into the computer, and sticks the other end onto her temples. Lisa passes Gabby into Daniel's arms, and he slips her into the tank.

Gabby bobbles in the murky green water like a buoy in the ocean. Reluctantly, Daniel closes the lid and turns back to type furiously into the computer, pausing only to readjust his glasses.

"Activation takes twenty minutes," Daniel says to Lisa once the sequence initiates.

"Where will her consciousness go? Do you have a doll already made?" Lisa doesn't speak with conviction anymore. She's out of her element—she's scared, timid, *worried.*

"Of course I have a doll for her," Daniel snaps. "I'll retrieve it momentarily."

Lisa clears her throat. "Is it true? My parents asked you to… to cure me?"

Daniel nods. "At a cost, I should tell you. This equipment is expensive." He pauses. "I suppose you want to see if they've gotten their money's worth?"

Lisa mimics Daniel by folding her arms and shrugging, so as not to commit to an answer. Daniel looks her up and down, his resentment unyielding. Eventually, he sniffs and walks towards another monitor, his movements rigid—his body's reaction to an unwelcome task. That, I still remember.

"Give me your hand," he says harshly, fumbling with a large needle. Lisa flinches when the scarlet liquid burbles up on her skin. He squeezes a few droplets onto one of his scanners and waits for the blue light confirmation to flash. Even with my returned memories, I still can't name or describe his equipment—it all looks the same. Silver, shiny, and relatively large.

"Here," he says rudely, handing her a cotton ball. "Dab off the excess."

"What did you need my blood for?" Lisa shakily presses the cotton to her wound.

Daniel motions at the machine. Numbers flicker wildly on the small screen until they settle into: "5TATU5: CUR3D".

"Does it…" Lisa bends over to read the screen, squinting her eyes against the glare.

"Yes." Daniel says. "You're finished. Done. I don't have to manage you anymore. You can find your own way home because I'm certainly not wasting any more time."

Lisa cradles the cotton ball close to her chest and looks to me for reassurance.

"Don't look at me," I bark. "Be grateful you're alive and healthy. Just don't mess it up this time."

"I didn't even know I was sick…" Lisa whispers, her eyes watering. "I'm so sorry. I didn't understand. I only remembered the good things. I didn't know I was…I didn't know I *am*…"

"Honestly, Lisa, shut up." I shake my head. "We get it. You're a dumb person, and you've done stupid things. Rather than complain about it, *fix* it. You were a broken doll, but you're not a broken human. Get your act together."

"Ella," Daniel hushes. "Don't be like that."

"I *am* like that!" I'm also tired of sitting on the floor like an idiot. "She's cured! She's cured after inflicting this on herself. She's cured after terrorizing me. She's cured after the turmoil she put her loved ones through. Yay for Lisa, she's *cured*! The bad guys *always* win!"

No one responds. No one ever does when I'm in human form. I'm not as cute or polite as the doll I was in.

"I'm sorry," Lisa says, her eyes focused on the floor. She awkwardly bows and runs through the door, her footsteps slapping the stairs. When the front door clicks closed, I know it's the last time I'll ever see Lisa.

Daniel steadily walks towards me, about to sit me up on the stool he rolls over.

"Stop," I hiss, waving him away. "I'll be fine here."

"You can't sit on the floor like that," he says softly, his eyebrows puckered. "You're soaked, and, and there's glass everywhere!"

"I'm fine," I mutter, glancing down at my stubby fingers. "It gets harder to re-remember everything. I don't recall it being so emotionally difficult last time."

"That's what you said last time," Daniel smiles grimly, taking his place on the seat. He tents his fingers and fidgets, sighing as if it's going out of fashion. "I can't heal you, Ella. I told you that last time, too. And the times before that. I can cure illness easily—in fact, I think it's time I released it to the public—but, *physical* conditions like your spine…"

"Yes, it's not meant to be," I say with certainty, wiping away a rogue tear. "I was never meant to dance."

"I don't believe that!" Daniel grabs my hand to stroke it tenderly with his thumb.

"I don't believe in a lot of things—herbal medicine, hypnosis—but it doesn't mean they don't exist, does it?" I counter, squeezing his hand the same way I did on the night of the accident. "I have to get over myself. It's been thirty years. I never see my son because I'm too obsessed with being a dancing doll. Was this the first time I met Gabby? I don't remember her…"

"You met her six years ago, when you returned to your human form for nine months. Since then, I told her that you moved to Florida to be with your sister, just so she doesn't continually ask me where Grandma is. That was the last time you spoke to Jason."

"*Really?*" Surely, it hasn't been six years since I saw my son! "Was that when we had that fight?"

Daniel purses his lips so tightly, they're barely visible.

"Oh…" I vaguely recall the day Jason said he never wanted to see me again. Maybe, I blocked out that memory, or maybe, it's just taking a while for it to come back. It's like having perpetual, yet fleeting, amnesia. "Remind me; did he not want to see me because I was a doll?"

"You were human when you fought." Daniel sweeps my hair behind my ear. "He understood my experiment and how it helped others, but he... he said you were selfish and ungrateful for continuously wiping your memory to live a life free of responsibility."

"And when did he come to you about Gabby?"

"It was only last week. This epidemic is *nearly* universally fatal to O Positive blood types. We knew Gabby would die, so he asked if I could help. He's experimenting with medical cures too, but he's not having any success. I've considered showing him how to transfer consciousness. It'd be great if he followed in my footsteps." Daniel coughs into his fist. "I'm hoping Gabby will only need to go under for a week, at most. I've found a new technique that shortens the timespan. Libby will be cured in three days. It's revolutionary, dear. It'll be nice to have the money, and I'm thrilled to be saving lives... and yet, despite all the good I've done... I still failed *you*." He chokes on the words and slumps over. I don't expect him to break down into tears like he does, and I'm even more confused when he throws himself off the chair and snuggles into me, resting his head on my lap. I struggle to feel sympathy for Daniel. I suppose the whole 'loving him' part hasn't returned to me yet. Truth be told, I'm far too busy pitying myself. After all, *he* was the one behind the wheel. *He* is the reason why I can never dance again.

"Can't you just put my consciousness into another human?"

"You asked me this last time." Daniel straightens, wiping away his tears and the lingering moisture from my time in the tank that's still weighing down my clothing. "I told you there are moral implications for that. I think religions and legal systems would agree with me."

I huff. "Let's not argue the semantics." I pause, thinking that

Daniel might reply. When he doesn't, I change the subject. "Why did you make it possible for dolls to cry?"

Daniel bites the inside of his mouth. "It's part of a separate experiment. I inserted tear ducts and small amounts of water inside the doll's head. I wanted to see if it was possible to convey physical emotion through an inanimate object. It was successful, which means bright possibilities for future studies."

I roll my eyes. I'm nothing but a guinea pig. "I met Sianne. You're a jerk for sending her to spy on me."

Daniel's eyes widen. "I didn't send her to spy on you!"

"Yes, you did! That's how you knew I was at the ballet–or when I hurt myself outside! Don't lie! I'm sick of the lies!"

"Fine! I didn't trust you!" Daniel's shakes when he inhales. "Sianne was worrying about her mortality, so I offered to turn her into a doll on one condition: that she watch you when I wasn't around. I was so worried about you breaking that I needed someone to be my eyes. But her mind didn't cope with the transition, and I lost her. Then I found her, and then I lost her again…"

"That's because she deliberately hid from you. Lisa found her locked in a box. She's absolutely mental, now. She kept telling me 3-4-7-8-1-9-2. She said it was the code to her lab."

"It's not." Daniel sighs. "It's our bloody lotto numbers. Where is she now?"

I shrug and motion towards the cupboard. "I'm guessing the miniature shadow in the corner belongs to her. She's doing what she does best; *spying* on me."

The shadow darts behind a box when Sianne realizes she's been spotted. Daniel shakes his head and follows her until he manages to run her to ground.

"No!" she squeals, kicking and punching his hand. "The trolls want my money! They said it's infected!"

Daniel purses his lips and grunts as he snaps Sianne over his knee. She stops moving instantly, the green mist wafting into the cool stale air. He drops her remains to the ground and hurries towards one of the tubes. Inside, a woman our age has just woken up. She thrashes in the water, her cheeks expanding like a pufferfish's as she waits for Daniel to set her loose. Eventually, he presses the button on the side, and the water drains. Sianne gasps for air and leans against the tube while she catches her breath. I'm a bit annoyed. All Lisa had to do was press a button, and I would've avoided slicing my skin on the broken glass. What do they say? Hindsight is always 20/20.

"What happened?" Sianne coughs, her teeth chattering.

"I'm bringing you back to reality," Daniel offers his hand so Sianne can gracefully exit the tube. She rubs her arms in an attempt to warm up, then steps out onto the dingy floorboards.

"Of course!" Her eyes roll back so only the whites show. She looks as weak as I feel. "Ella started remembering…"

The professor flinches and hands her another spare lab coat. "We'll talk later. Why don't you go freshen up outside for a moment? Once I help Gabby, I'll tend to you."

"Gabby?" Sianne wrings out her hair, so thin, she's almost balding.

"Your niece," Daniel clarifies. "It might take a while for your memories to snap into place."

Sianne closes her eyes, small creases lacing her drooping skin when she tightens them. "Daniel, my mind is so muddled. Sounds and sights are reversed. My memories are like a dream. I don't fear death now. I think it will be less confusing…" She pauses. "Daniel, Ella is beyond repair. You can't keep her as a doll. You both need to let go."

Daniel tugs on her, trying to lead her away. She's a bigger woman, a lot like me, so he struggles.

"Daniel, will my mind ever go back to normal?" She gently rubs her temples with her index fingers. "Life is clouded."

"I can't guarantee that it will, Sianne," Daniel says softly. "I'm sorry I pulled you into this. I just wanted Ella to enjoy a world of ignorance and bliss. I thought you could help protect her. I thought she'd be happier that way. That you both would."

"She'd have been happier knowing the truth," Sianne mumbles, finally shifting when Daniel pulls on her arm. He leads her out of the room, closing the door behind her. I wish I had something cogent to say, but really, what is there? He'd known turning her into a doll without the benefit of induced amnesia was bound to backfire. So, he'd gone and deliberately ruined his sister's life to try and appease me. He's always done that, though. He always put me first. Just ask Jason.

"Thank you for your patience, my love," Daniel says, crouching next to me. He tilts his head and caresses my face.

"Time is all I have." I dab at the blood seeping from a cut on my hand. "You're quite good at ruining people's lives, you know. First mine, now your sister's. Bravo."

He goes to say something, then clears his throat. "Why do you hate me so much?"

"I don't hate you." My gaze drops to my useless legs.

"Don't lie to me." Lowered, his voice sounds almost manly.

I glance up at him and allow my icy gaze to bore into his soul. "What do you want me to say? Obviously, I resent you, Daniel!" I strangle the air with my hands and slump over. "You ruined me! You *broke* me."

"I've done everything I can to try and fix it! I don't know what else I can do!"

"Nothing," I snap, "unless you transfer my consciousness into a character in a book. I mean, that'd be ideal. I could finally escape you."

We turn our heads when something beeps loudly. Gabby's activation must be complete.

Daniel's face is pained, and he looks torn between staying with me to hash out our problems and helping Gabby. Eventually, he stands and heads for the wooden box, pulling out a Gabby doll.

She looks nothing like her human form–I suppose Daniel must've been in a rush. Her hair is outrageously long and messily sewn together. Her eyes are the wrong color and she's wearing overalls–something Gabby would never be caught dead in. She squirms in Daniel's grip and studies the lab like babies do in new surroundings. He lowers her onto one of the counters and smiles.

"Hello, Gabby. I'm the professor. You probably can't remember much, but I promise that will be temporary. I'm here to help you. I'm here to *fix* you. Do you think you can let me do that?"

Gabby reluctantly nods, scanning the area. "Why is there glass on the floor? Was there an earthquake?"

"Yes." Daniel scoops Gabby into his arms. "But we're okay now. I'm going to introduce you to the treasure chest, which I think you will find most comfortable. You'll meet Libby, whom you'll also like."

He shields Gabby's eyes from where I sit and takes her out of the lab. I sit impatiently, twiddling my thumbs and wringing my shirt. Good grief, I'm fat. I forgot how big I was. Nothing but gross flubber.

When Daniel returns, he completely ignores me and heads straight to the computer. His fingers are a blur on the keyboard, and his glasses keep slipping down his nose.

"Oh my God!" he exclaims. He raises his hands triumphantly and hops awkwardly on one foot. "Oh my God! Her condition is stabilizing! She's already improving! I did it! *I DID IT!*"

Daniel skips towards me and takes me by the hands, his face flushed and youthful.

"Congratulations," I say half-heartedly. "So she's no longer terminal?"

"She will still take a while to heal," Daniel puffs, resting one hand on his chest to calm down, "but I think she'll be okay! I checked Libby as well. She's rapidly improving! I have to call Jason! Gabby will be able to go home next week and then… then I'll have to publish my findings! There will be no sickness in the world!"

"There will *always* be sickness." I pull my hand from his. "Once we eradicate one illness, a stronger one will emerge. Daniel, this is *nonsense*. You can't go to world governments and scientists telling them you know how to cure the epidemic. How will they believe that you transferred a mind into a doll? This *can't* go mainstream. You need to keep it between friends and family like you're doing now. There will be too much controversy."

Daniel stares at me in disgust, like I have something offensive on my face. "I can't believe you. I found a revolutionary, non-invasive cure—"

"—*non-invasive?*" I shriek. "You've *got* to be kidding me, Daniel! It's the most invasive thing you can think of! You wipe their memories... you *control* memories in case we start to recall something... and you turn us into vulnerable dollies! It's mental!"

"It *works* though," he says through gritted teeth.

"Well, not for everyone." I cross my arms and stare at the mess on the floor that used to be the tube I've been living in (on and off) for the past thirty years. "Put me back."

Daniel hangs his head and speaks to the floor. "I don't want to do this anymore, Ella. I want my wife back. I'm sick of caring for you as a doll, only for you to *continuously* grow suspicious of your former life. We've relived this pattern more times than I can count."

"You don't? I don't want to be like this. I'm a fat, old woman. I like being young and free. Put me back."

"No," he says. I don't know why he's being as stubborn as me today.

"*Put me back!*" I scream. I try to crawl towards the tubes to do it myself, but Daniel easily stops me by pulling on my waist. "*Please*, Daniel. This time, I don't want to know I had a human life—just let me think I'm *really* a doll. Oh, but don't introduce me to anymore psychopaths like Lisa. She was crazy when she was human, but something about your experiment really pushed her over the edge."

Daniel frowns. "Do you understand how selfish you're being? You'd rather forget about your son, your husband, and your granddaughter and permanently live life as a doll?"

I nod. I'm already tired of my back aching and my vision blurring. I don't like feeling cold and wet, and I don't like how heavy my entire body feels. Nothing about my human form is appealing anymore. Least of all, Daniel.

"Just wait," he says, speaking higher than he usually does. "How about I get you a banana? Or, or, I'll cook a nice roast and we can have chocolate mousse afterwards! While you wait, you can soak in a hot bath with scented candles and read a good book! You're only saying this because you're cold and in pain, which I understand! But, but, you don't have to revert! Please dear, just stay with me this time. We can make it work!"

Part of me pities Daniel, but most of me doesn't care. I want my old life back–my life as a young, dancing doll. I'm nicer as a doll, anyway. "I don't want to make it work." I enunciate, catching his eyes. "I'm over it. Over *you*. I was happier not knowing."

"But Ella..." his voice shakes, and his face droops. "Ella, I love you so much. I just want to have a normal life with you. I promise, we can make it good. We can all celebrate next week when Gabby is healthy! Jason and his wife will visit, and we'll have a lovely meal and play board games! Please, Ella, I, I just can't *lose* you again."

I lift my chin. "You've already lost me. The moment that car swerved and ejected me through the window. The moment you chose to experiment on me. I've made my decision. It's time you move on, Daniel."

"Sweetie-pie..." Daniel's voice croaks.

I inhale steadily, and coldly pat my husband's head like an animal's. I stare at him intently and make sure my words are firm and final.

"Put me back."

CHAPTER TWENTY-FOUR

COULD WE START AGAIN. PLEASE?

Lovely music plays softly outside the treasure chest. It's sweet, contemporary, and very calming.

My room has altered slightly–the professor said it was time for a change, so he redecorated it to match the room of a TV show I like to watch. It's a lot more modern, with more greys and whites instead of pinks and purples. The professor said it was 'time for me to grow-up'–whatever that means.

He took all my tutus away and replaced them with an array of dresses, gowns, and pantsuits. I'm happy about the decision–for some reason, I'm a little over tutus.

There's a large recorder that sits in the corner of the treasure chest. The professor mentioned that I might like to record 'imagination time'. I rewound the huge tape to see if there were any other recordings on it, but it was completely blank.

I've only been in existence for a month. It's a good month.

The attic is fetching, really. It's rustic, but I like it. The floorboards are covered with various red and fluffy rugs and portraits hang from the freshly-painted white walls. Red curtains complement the rugs, and the professor brought in a plasma TV and a grey couch yesterday.

He said it was something about 'moving on' or… or *something*. I don't really know what he means, but that doesn't bother me. I remember him painting the walls and cleaning up piles of junk in the corner. He didn't look at me much for the first few days I came into existence. Whenever I spoke to him, he put his head down and left the room. I worried I offended him, but he's a lot brighter now. He's much happier and quite chatty.

"Ella? Ella?" Gabby enters the attic. She spots me in the treasure chest and bounds over. I like Gabby. She's the professor's granddaughter and visits from time to time. She was very pale when I met her a month ago—she looked sickly, but now she's vibrant and full of energy. She's wearing yellow today—yellow suits her olive skin.

"Gabby!" I grin when she bends over to lift me up. "Are you taking me down the slide today?"

"I sure am! Grandpa doesn't seem to mind you going outside anymore. He's a lot more… like, lax with you now. Actually, he's a lot cooler with me as well."

I cock my head to the side, confused. "What do you mean? He's always let me do whatever I want. I mean, I'm only a month old, but still!"

Gabby frowns and then shakes her head and grins. "Oh," her voice is high, like she's lying, "of course! Silly me. Let's go!"

She holds onto me as she skips down the stairs and bursts through the sliding door into the backyard. It must be spring, because birds are chirping and flowers are blooming. I love the outdoors. The professor often lets me play in the garden, so long as it's not raining. He even let Gabby take me for a bike ride yesterday.

Gabby lowers me into the sandpit and builds a castle for me to play on. I climb on top of it and raise my hands in the air.

"I'm the Queen of the castle!" I declare dramatically.

Gabby laughs and bows down before me. "Oh, your majesty! What will your first law be?"

"I declare," I say in a deep, royal voice, "that Gabby shall visit me *every* day of the week!"

"Yes, your majesty!" she says with another deep curtsy.

We laugh together as the professor joins us from the kitchen, bringing out a fizzing lemonade for Gabby. He's holding a second one that he sips on for himself. He's not in his lab coat today–he's dressed in fitted jeans and a lovely collared shirt.

"Oh-la-la!" Gabby pouts like a model. "What are you all dressed up for, Grandpa?"

He blushes and tugs on the collar of his neck. "My dear, if you *must* know… I have a lunch date with an old lady friend."

Gabby and I gasp in unison.

"But what about Grandma?" Gabby coughs, almost dropping her lemonade.

"Grandma has gone to a better place," the professor says quietly, smiling sweetly towards me. "It's time I moved on."

Gabby glances at me, almost sympathetically, or like she knows something. She shakes her head and then pats the professor on the back and speaks in a poor English accent. "Good for you, ol' chap! Where are you takin' the missus to?"

The professor laughs his breathy laugh. "Sushi. It's been a while since I've enjoyed tuna wrapped in seaweed!"

"It sounds like you've earned it!" I chime in. "You seem like such a lovely man, but you're always in that lab! It's about time you got out and found the love of your life!"

"Yes," the professor says almost nostalgically. "But I will always love my broken doll." He bows the same way Gabby did, and I curtsy in return. "Sweetheart, your father is in the living room–he'll be watching you while I'm gone. Have fun, girls."

"We will!" we reply in unison.

"You make sure you have fun on your date!" I add.

The professor stops at the sliding door and strokes the edge of it tenderly. He looks at us with watery eyes, even though he is smiling. I can't understand how he can look both sad and happy at the same time. I ought to hug him, so I make my descent from my castle and begin to toddle over. Before I reach the edge of the sandpit, he has already turned on his heel and closed the door, his fingerprints smearing the glass.

"I'm happy for him," Gabby says as she creates a new wall for my castle. I turn slowly and sit next to her. "I only ever met Grandma once, and she was really bitter. I've never seen Grandpa so... I don't know, energized or something. He signed up with a big medical corporation last week to show his studies, so maybe that's why. Either way, he looks good."

I nod in agreement. "He really does. He takes good care of us, doesn't he?"

"Definitely. We had a few arguments when I was sick, but that was a tense time for everyone. I now understand what he was trying to do for us... I mean, for me. I sure do love him."

I don't reply, but I make sure to duck when Gabby overthrows the sand bucket over my head. I push it off and poke my tongue out at her, and she dissolves in giddy chuckles.

As we play, we're distracted by the sliding door rolling open. Dressed in jeans and a collared shirt, a man stands at the door, tense and nervous.

"Hey, Dad!" Gabby calls. "Come play with us!"

Reluctantly, he shoves his hands into his jean pockets and joins us in the sand. He watches me, his jaw clenched and his lips pursed. He's ridiculously handsome in that brooding sort of way. He looks a lot like the professor—high cheekbones, similar eyes, and sharp nose, with only his thick hair still black and a widow's peak to set him apart.

"Hello, Jason." I offer my tiny hand for him to shake. He doesn't accept. "It's lovely to officially meet you."

Jason scoffs and builds a doorway for the castle. "Ella, do you know how I chose Gabby's name?" His tone drips with… disdain? Though, what for? When I shake my head, he continues. "Your full name is Gabriella, and I thought that by naming my daughter Gabrielle, it might help her grandmother bond with her. I hoped it would bring her back to us."

I frown. What on earth is he talking about?

"Dad," Gabby says. "Stop."

"I was wrong, of course. She was too wrapped up in her selfish ways to care about her family. After a while, she didn't even care that she left me. I was fortunate that the rest of my family loved me enough." Jason watches me carefully. "They were all I needed. They taught me about morals, decency, and kindness. The best thing I ever took away from them was learning how to forgive. Bitterness and anger consumes you, and I'm tired of punishing myself for her selfishness."

My eyes squeak awkwardly when I dart them from Gabby to Jason. Is this about his father's new lady friend?

"I forgive her," Jason says quietly, cracking a very small, but a very certain smile. "To understand all, you must forgive all. I think I understand her, now." He gently picks me up and kisses my head. "Through all of the heartache and neglect, I understand."

He scratches his ear and laughs, before standing and walking back into the house. I bug my eyes at Gabby.

"What was *that* about?"

Gabby clears her throat and shrugs. "Ah, you know. Adults. You'll probably work it out later. Shall we finish our masterpiece?"

While we build the remainder of the castle, I think about what Gabby said earlier. I've only known the professor for a month, but he is very thoughtful. He redesigned my treasure chest and ensured that I have everything I could possibly want. He sat down and painted a portrait of Gabby and me and taught me about the endangered animals. He takes care of his sister Sianne, who lives in the guest room. She's a little odd and talks to herself, but he treats her the same way he treats us. He always puts everyone's needs before his own, even when he's sad.

Maybe it's too soon for me to admit it to myself, much less to Gabby, but a flutter in my chest makes itself known whenever I see the professor. I never feel cold, hungry, sore – I don't think I *can* feel anything, except for the warm flicker of hope that lives in my heart for the people who surround me.

I think they call it love.

A TASTE OF
SHATTERED GIRLS
BY TYROLIN PUXTY

SHATTERED GIRLS

I used to like watching the sunsets on the beach. But it's not fun anymore. How could it be, when Gabby curls her knees to her chest and sobs for half an hour? It's heartbreaking.

I wish she could be happy and play with me. She told me that I spent years trapped in an attic until she took me to live with her, but I can't remember that time. I don't know what it's like to not cartwheel in the sand and run from the tide nipping at my ankles. Why wouldn't anyone be happy with that kind of freedom?

"Gabby?" I ask, my pointe shoes leaving circular prints in the sand. I rest my hands on her knee, startled by how smooth her shaven legs are. I forget she ages. She was ten when we met, but that was five years ago. Her cheeks are narrower, her hair is shorter, and her voice is maturing. She tries to make me age with her, but I don't know why. Every March 31st, she wishes me a Happy Birthday and paints my face to look slightly older. She detaches my limbs and replaces them with longer ones, but I'm probably only half an inch taller after four birthdays.

"Go play, Ella," Gabby sniffs, wiping away tears. "Make up new choreography."

"I don't feel like dancing today." I climb into her lap when she stretches out her legs. Just because I'm dressed in a multicolored leotard and tutu, doesn't mean I always want to dance.

Gabby doesn't respond; instead she hiccups and strokes my bun. The seagulls overhead temporarily drown out her sobs, but her chest still heaves with each unsteady breath.

"Why do you still beat yourself up?" My neck creaks when I look up at her. That's one annoying thing about being a doll. "It's been three months. It's not a big deal."

"It's a huge deal!" she snaps, gulping the later spring air. "I exposed you! I exposed the family secret! If Grandpa found out…" She stares at the waves.

"The professor won't find out," I say unsympathetically, a little tired of reassuring her. "He left us. He left us to be a bigshot scientist. Besides, I don't care that people know. I can sit on your desk and learn things at school now. I hated being in that cramped bag and peeking through the pockets."

"You're just lucky people think you were a robot. If anyone knew you were human—"

"—they won't." I pat her thumb. "People just think you have the coolest toy in the world that can help with homework."

Gabby cracks a small smile and picks up sand, running it through the gaps in her fingers. "It was Devin's fault, you know. I had no idea she was filming."

I shrug. "I went viral on the internet. It's every teenager's dream!"

"But you're not a teenager…" Gabby mumbles, sweeping her golden hair behind her ear. It's the same color as the sun's reflection on the waves. I like it.

I don't reply. Gabby's been particularly snappy lately, so I don't want to aggravate her further. She sniffs, tracing her fingers in the sand. "Let's go. Dinner's almost on."

"What are you having?"

"Whatever the parents decide." She lifts me onto her shoulder.

It makes me feel like a parrot on a pirate. "It's Wednesday, so probably spaghetti."

"Spaghetti looks messy."

"That's half the allure."

Gabby trudges through the sand, visibly saddened to leave behind the calming waves. I'm not–after all, there's always tomorrow.

She ungracefully shuffles up the cement stairs until we hit the road. The street is empty, and the stores are closed. It's amazing how quickly the world shuts down.

"I don't want to go home." Gabby kicks a pebble. "Pam and Jason will be at each other's throats again."

"I wish you wouldn't call them that," I say quietly, adjusting my hand so it fits in the stump better.

"It's the only way to grab their attention lately."

"They're not here now," I say, "so you don't need to call them that. They're your parents; you should treat them as such."

"And you're…" Her eyes flash when she turns to look at me, her frown turning sympathetic. She sighs and shakes her head. "No one's who they think they are."

I don't know what she means. She may just be depressed. Should I find some pills in the medicine cabinet? One of them is bound to help.

"Can we walk down Main Street?" I shift uncomfortably when Gabby turns into a dimly lit street.

"Why?"

"Because the TV reported six local girls missing last night. I don't want you to be one of them."

She pauses at the intersection. She knows I have a point. Her usual shortcut shaves ten minutes off our walk, but it's not a crowded area. If we take Main Street, there will be lights and people–two things that make darkness less terrifying. Reluctantly, she turns around and continues down Main Street, tucking her hands into her hoodie pockets.

Riding Gabby is what it must be like to ride a giant elephant or camel. Her strides are unpredictable and bumpy, so I have to hold onto her ear for balance. No one looks at me. The town is used to Gabby having a "robot" on her shoulder.

"You know, I don't think you've changed much," I say when we glimpse our reflections in a sparkling storefront.

"What do you mean?"

"Well, you're taller and lankier, but you still look the same. It must be nice to grow. You know, like, naturally."

"It's not nice at all." She turns the corner onto a street with only two streetlights. Our street.

"Why isn't it nice?"

Gabby kicks at the gravel, her trainers wearing at the toe. I can tell she's unsettled by how still the night is. "Being a kid is fun, and I think being an adult could be all right. It's just this middle stage. People are confused, mean, and dumb. Plus boys are all ugly at this age. Their noses get too big for their face, or something."

I giggle, excited that she's managed to make a joke. Surely, depressed people don't do that. That's why the comedians on TV are so funny; they're too happy to be sad. "Big noses mean you'll make lots of money. That's what the psychic told the man on TV."

"That's probably what she said to make him feel better," she says, covering her mouth when she laughs. I love it when she laughs.

"I doubt it. TV is always right, haven't you heard?"

She stops laughing and comes to an abrupt halt on our lawn, gaping at the front door.

"Why is our door open?" I ask.

"I don't know."

"Why are all the lights turned off?"

"I don't know."

"Why aren't we going in?"

Gabby swallows. "Because I'm scared of what I'll find."

I climb onto her head to get a better view. She'd barely feel me there. "Want me to investigate?"

"No." She takes a moment to breathe. "We go in together."

I take hold of her hair like reins, keeping my voice low. "I'm with you."

She doesn't move. If I was watching this on TV, I'd guess the scene was paused.

"I think I'm stuck in a dream." Gabby's voice is tight. "The lawn is miles long, Ella. Nothing makes sense, it's... it's all in slow-motion. It's like I'm a doll again."

"It's your anxiety." I calmly stroke her braid. I can't feel how soft it must be, but, at least, she can feel me. "Maybe we should call the police?"

"No," she says, inhaling but not exhaling. She crosses the lawn and stands in the doorway, staring into the house. No lights are on.

"Breathe, Gabby. Breathe for both of us."

Gabby nods and steps in, the floorboards creaking beneath her. I always liked how Gabby's parents kept the traditional feel to the house with polished flooring and high ceilings, but it's strange without them here. Our home doesn't feel like home anymore.

"Stay here," I say, "I'll tell you when the coast is clear."

I sneak through the hall, poking my head around each corner before entering the next room. I figure it's best for me to go first— if the intruders are still here, they're not going to do much harm to a doll.

No one is in the living room, or the bedrooms. The windows are open, and the curtains float delicately in the breeze.

If the intruders are still here, they're masters of disguise.

"Gabby?" I call. She enters, eyes wide and nostrils flared.

"Why are the windows open?" She twirls her hoodie's cords.

I shrug. "Maybe your parents wanted fresh air?"

"Their cars are still in the driveway." Her voice trembles. "Why would they leave everything wide open like this if everything was okay?"

The house pipes suddenly clank when the dishwasher switches on. Gabby clutches at her heart and utters an obscenity. "Have you checked the kitchen?"

I shake my head. Gabby pushes past me, the kitchen door swinging when she moves through. I follow suit, unsettled by the number of knives sprawled across the counter. One of the chairs has been knocked over, along with a bowl of fruit.

I kick at a bruised grape. "Oh no!" I run towards the back door, my eyes clicking with each blink.

"What?" Gabby asks.

I don't respond as I poke my head through the cat-flap and check the backyard for intruders.

"Jupiter?" I press my plastic lips together to make a kissing sound. "Jupes?"

When the inky cat doesn't come, I walk towards Gabby, dragging my feet.

"The cat's gone," I say quietly while Gabby inspects one of the knives.

"Cats don't always come when you call them," she says, but it doesn't sound like she's listening. She inspects a banana, which is peeled and squished. "Someone's taken my parents."

"And your cat." I run back towards the flap to double-check. "Come on, Jupes!"

"Come on, Ella." Gabby bends over to pick me up and places me on her head. "We're leaving."

"Where to?" I ask, devastated to leave Jupes behind. I used to hate cats, but I've grown somewhat obsessed.

"Aunt Sianne's."

If I could gulp, I would. "But she's mental. Can't we go to your friend's house?"

"This is a family matter." Gabby tears down the hallway like a whirlwind. She goes into her room and pulls out random items of clothing, shoving them into her backpack. "Could you get my toothbrush, please?"

I don't hesitate. I jump from her head, the forced landing enough to make my ankles squeak, but not enough to break. I hurry into the bathroom across the hall and climb the sink. I stumble on the drawers and note that the medicine drawer has been ransacked. The only thing left is the aspirin. How odd.

Her toothbrush is about the same height as me, so it's awkward to carry it out. When I return, Gabby stares at a photograph of the four of us at the Great Barrier Reef. She'd spent weeks sewing a scuba suit for me, just so I felt included. It was sweet.

"Are you ready?"

Gabby flinches when I speak, pulling her gaze away from the photo. "Yeah." She grabs the toothbrush and picks me up, swifter and rougher than usual. "Did you find anything in there?"

I pause. "No. The bathroom was just like normal." I'm not good at lying, but Gabby is too flustered to notice. I don't know why I didn't tell her. Didn't want her to worry, I guess? Her dad is a medical scientist, just like the professor, so the thought of intruders stealing medicine just seems like an unnecessary stress.

We leave what was once our home, but Gabby doesn't shut the front door behind us. I guess she's not ready to close the chapter on her parents just yet.

THE STORY CONTINUES IN

SHATTERED GIRLS

BY TYROLIN PUXTY

COMING IN 2016 FROM

CURIOSITY
QUILLS PRESS

ABOUT THE AUTHOR

I'm a Jack, or more accurately, a Tyrolin of all trades.

In my 23 years, I have:

- walked the red carpet for song nominations
- was awarded the Australia Day award in 2014 for Music and in 2015 for the Arts
- worked as a qualified paralegal
- appeared in TV Shows
- hired for product photography
- modelled
- became a Justice of the Peace
- started my own club for school children interested in the arts
- worked for a successful magazine company
- published a book
- hugged a koala
- and had a show ride collapse on my head

THANK YOU
FOR READING

Please visit http://curiosityquills.com/reader-survey
to share your reading experience with the author of
this book!

Sweet Dreams are Made of Teeth, by Richard Roberts

How does a nightmare hunt? He tracks your dreams into the Light, and chases them into the Dark. How does a nightmare love? With passion and obsession and lust and amazement. How does a nightmare grow up? With pain and grief and doubt and kindness and learning and dedication and courage. First Fang hunted, now he loves, and soon he'll have to grow up.

Virtual Immortality, by Matthew Cox

Nina Duchenne walked away from a perfect life to pursue a noble idea, but one tragic night shatters her dreams. Joey Dillon lives on a perpetual adrenaline rush. A self-styled cyber cowboy chasing thrills wherever he can find them, he is unconcerned with what will happen twenty minutes into the future. Voices from beyond the grave distract Nina from her pursuit of two international terrorists, and send Joey on a mission to find out who is playing games, putting the fate of the entire West City, as well as Nina's humanity, at risk.

Unhappenings, by Edward Aubry

When Nigel Walden is fourteen, the UNHAPPENINGS begin. Several years later, when Nigel is visited by two people from his future, he hopes they can explain why the past keeps rewriting itself around him. His search for answers takes him fifty-two years forward in time, where he finds himself stranded and alone. And then he meets Helen. Equal parts time-travel adventure and tragic love story, Unhappenings is a tale of gravely bad choices, and Nigel's struggle not to become what he sees in the preview of his worst self.

Automatic Woman, by Nathan L. Yocum

The London of 1888, the London of steam engines, Victorian intrigue, and horseless carriages is not a safe place nor simple place…but it's his place. Jolly is a thief catcher, a door-crashing thug for the prestigious Bow Street Firm, assigned to track down a life sized automatic ballerina.

But when theft turns to murder and murder turns to conspiracy, can Jolly keep his head above water? Can a thief catcher catch a killer?